£8.00 =
S←

CW00953836

MAROONED IN THE CREEKS

THE NIGER DELTA MEMOIRS

J.H.O. OLOWE

iUniverse, Inc.
New York   Bloomington

Marooned in the Creeks
The Niger Delta Memoirs

This is a work of fiction. All of the characters, names, incidents, organizations, and dialogue in this novel are either the products of the author's imagination or are used fictitiously.

iUniverse books may be ordered through booksellers or by contacting:

iUniverse
1663 Liberty Drive
Bloomington, IN 47403
www.iuniverse.com
1-800-Authors (1-800-288-4677)

ISBN: 978-1-4502-7580-4 (sc)
ISBN: 978-1-4502-7582-8 (hc)
ISBN: 978-1-4502-7581-1 (ebk)

Printed in the United States of America

iUniverse rev. date: 12/28/2011

To all who long, and work for the development
of the riverine communities of Nigeria.

CHAPTER ONE

First person narrative

"*I beg o Oga make you enter, I wan go,*" the boat skipper bellowed. Goddy, as his mates called him, was a very massive individual, and from the way the boat rocked each time he stepped on it, he must be pretty heavy. Much of his tall frame has been consumed by his generous mien. He carried a bulky and expansive chest on which he spotted a coconut-sized head. If he had a neck at all, it was not visible to the onlooker, as his massive torso has sucked it in. His deep guttural voice complemented his out-of- the- ordinary appearance. Each time he stood on the passageway, there was always a line-up behind him, because his frame and girth took the entire space.

Samuel Audu, my partner and I met Goddy at a *peppersoup* joint the previous evening. He had come to Yenagoa on a leg of his regular shuttle between Warri and Yenagoa. He carried, and distributed supplies among the workers of an oil company locations scattered over the Niger delta.

In spite of his scary look, he was a very amiable individual. He exuded warmth and cool. He spoke some mangled Yoruba, and ever since he discovered I was Yoruba, he insisted I spoke to him in Yoruba. He ignored all my entreaties, including the fact that my partner, Samuel, was not Yoruba. According to him, he had lived in Lagos years ago. It was the sudden death of his brother,

1

a sailor with a national shipping company that cut short his stay in Lagos. He still nursed the idea of living in Lagos, and as soon he was able to make enough savings from his present job, *"alele* Lagos", he said gleefully.

We had even engaged in friendly beer - parlour discussion before we knew his identity. Since Ukubie was along his route, he promised to give us a ride. Naturally, we demonstrated our appreciation by buying him and his friends a couple of bottles of beer. It was not our plan to leave Yenagoa the following day, but the offer of a ride in the 'comfort' of an oil company's cargo boat was a godsend, and too tempting to ignore.

We arrived at the jetty very early, and stayed at the agreed point, waiting for him. The waterside was a beehive of activities, and a picture of disorder and bewilderment. There were a number of boats and canoes. Two large jetties formed the centres of activities. Some boats were taking on passengers, while others were discharging their passengers and cargo. Some of them looked so rickety that I could not imagine how they managed to stay afloat. Canoes and smaller boats, which were more in number, did not bother to stay by the jetties, or did not have access to them, as the bigger boats had taken over the available space. They were tied to shrubs and sticks by the riverbank, or in some cases tied to other bigger boats. Goddy's boat, a large dinghy, painted bright pink, looked like an egret on a dunghill. Its bright crimson colour accentuated the overall squalor of the waterside backdrop. It was obvious it did not belong there, and Goddy demonstrated it amply in the unforthcoming way he addressed passengers, and many of them, who approached him for a ride, and the hasty manner he went about his preparation to leave the area. Written across the stern in black bold lettering was SEA TRUCK 1.

Along the riverbank was a small burgeoning market. Articles included items like firewood, palm oil, sugar cane and fish. Buyers skirted around the bank, and as each boat arrived, middlemen and women scrambled to welcome the passengers, and took custody of whatever commodities they brought, deferring the haggling and quibbling till the owners alighted from the boats. A small boy approached us with a basket full of live tilapia fish and crabs. I dismissed him with a negative shake of the head. He felt terribly disappointed, and still hovered around us for some time before finally giving up. As we were told later, 'educated' persons like us pay higher prices than the local folks, hence his persistence.

As it turned out, Goddy had other passengers apart from us. The practice seemed to be that on his return leg, when he had no regular cargo, he converted the boat to a commuter ferry. Prospective passengers clustered around him begging for space. At the end, there were fifteen passengers in all, men and women, including his assistant. The last passenger came in with some bags of cement, which were neatly stacked on some raised platform, and covered with a cellophane sheet. The presence of the cement on board gave me some worry, for I could not imagine how the boat would not sink with the weight. However, Goddy, sensing my apprehension, assured that the vessel was designed to take much more, and that he even needed such weight for stability. But it was obvious that the boat had more than it was designed to carry. The waterline was so precariously close that I could reach out and touch it from inside the boat. The owner of the cement also, noticing our disapproval, wasted no time in establishing some rapport with us. He must have assumed we were officials of the owner company.

We sat gingerly with trepidation on the aluminium sofa along the side panel of the boat. A woman, who sat by us on the same sofa, assured us of our safety, and even told us that we could rest our back on the panel. She demonstrated her point by leaning heavily on the panel, and the boat rocked in response. Moments earlier, she had trouble manoeuvring a large cane cage basket containing African grey parrots into the boat.

As soon as we settled down, we brought out our life jackets, and went into the ritual of putting them on. We had been issued one each in the orientation camp and warned never to travel on water without them. I inflated mine to make sure it was in good

3

condition. I finished in time to assist Samuel who had difficulty with his.

Two things struck us when we finally finished with the jackets, and looked up: First, all other passengers were staring at us as if we were kids playing with some strange toys, and second, the boat was not only underway, we were midstream; the boat was over a hundred feet away from the jetty. My fears about travelling on water surfaced in full force. I quickly closed my eyes and said my prayers silently.

"*Na wah o,*" Samuel intoned, holding firmly to the side panel in readiness for any eventuality, and looking blankly into space.

"What is that"? I asked vacuously.

"The boat is moving already!"

"I can...," I half said absent-mindedly, as the boat quivered violently, and sent me in rocking collision with the parrot woman. My apology to her must have been unexpected and therefore strange as she only looked at me and smiled. I was struggling to cope with the frightening expanse of water. I held on firmly to the bench, and closed my eyes in response to the giddiness that was already overtaking me.

"*Oga, no problem, alaaafia ni o!*" It was Goddy from the skipper's cabin. "*Hi safe pass moto!*"

"*Oga you never enter boat before?*" Another woman by my side said. The entire boat erupted in laughter. Several passengers offered one form of encouragement or the other either in the local language or Pidgin English.

"*Na where he go enter am? Na Lagos man e!*" Goddy said. Rather than elicit the usual laughter, the passengers started looking at us with curiosity. "*Na government send dem come here e.*"

Meanwhile, *Sea Truck* had attained full speed. The engine buzzed, and the boat, a planning vessel, surged along turbulently in response. Goddy in his skipper's cabin and the bow were at a higher level than the rest of us. The bow was now pointing skywards as if in readiness for a lift up, and the wake raced behind as if reaching out for some hidden object beneath the boat. The waves raced towards the banks, each trying to outdo the other. Some children swimming along the banks shouted and waved in appreciation as they welcomed the riptide and the entire turmoil in joyful extravagant splashes. Behind us, Yenagoa was shrinking and disappearing at a very fast rate.

"*O bye e*"! "*Sea Truck!*" The children chorused from the banks.

In a short while, the children were mere specks in the distance. The boat moved like a riot squad along the narrow river, sending the whole serene environment into disarray. However, if the children liked Sea Truck and its attendant commotion, it was not so with other travellers on the river. The movement of Sea Truck sent smaller boats and dinghies into jeopardy. If the boat had any warning signal at all, Goddy never used it. Each time we approached a canoe or a small boat Sea Truck, acting as the stand-on almighty all the time, slowed down, but at times not to a no-wake speed, and it was always as much as the unfortunate vessels could try not to overturn. The unlucky souls reacted by raining obscenities on Sea Truck. Goddy either took no notice of them, or tried to make fun out of it.

"*Na him dey make me fat*", or " *give am to your pikin*" or "*give am to your papa*", he would say. On one occasion, a canoe with some women paddlers did tip over, and characteristically, Goddy never thought it necessary to stop. It was more than we could bear.

"Stop!" I ordered in the manner of a police officer. I was on my feet. "What the hell do you think you are doing?" The sternness of my order won me a few supporters among fellow passengers as some of them pleaded with Goddy either to stop, or be careful. But to most of them, they could not be bothered, as it was a familiar experience. What was strange was our outlandish apprehension of it. As for Goddy, we could have been talking to a deaf-mute, as he merely looked back and shook his head.

"*Oga you no sabi dis people.*" It was Goddy after the unfortunate women were completely out of site. "*If to say I stop we for no leave dat place today e*".

"*Before you leave di place you go pay for di granmoder way don die twenty years before,*" Goddy's assistant added.

"*Na dat one concern you like my job,*" Goddy said in a carefree and distant manner.

"Must you kill other people to keep your job?" Samuel asked.

"*No be say I dey wicked. Di people sabi wetin dem dey do. As dey know say na company boat, dey fit tanda for road make di boat kill dem becos dey know say company go pay dem copesation. Copesation! Na hin dey behind everyting*". He laid emphasis on the word *copesation* (compensation), as if to confirm that the passengers were not familiar with it. "*Na so di person wey dey drive dis boat before los hin job. Na one Ogbenbiri man like dat. He hit one canoe like dat, and stop. As beke dey inside boat, he give di woman moni, copesation. When dey reach office nko. Wetin happen? Dey sack am.*".

"*Beke sak am! Amasoma pipu sabi dat kind ting propa,*" the assistant added.

"Then drive with more care." It was the only thing I could say after his explanation.

"*I dey try oga! Mo gbiyanju* Sir."

I managed a wry smile. Goddy's explanation concluded that episode, but the worst was yet to come. It was the pattern from Yenagoa to Ukubie.

The journey continued for a long time without any major incident. We were now fairly used to the experience. The initial fear seemed to have disappeared or, at least, gone under. The typical bumpy ride on rough surfaces no longer bordered us as they did initially, but we still had our life vests on in case of any eventuality. The only source of worry was the biting cold generated by the endless rain and draught. Goddy's assistant gave us a plastic sheet, which we used to cover our legs. It was large enough to cover our entire body, but it was so grimy we could not stand the touch of it on our dresses. He read us loud and clear, for he later advised us to use extra clothing from our luggage, which we did.

It was 1979, political activities were just taking off and political parties were being formed. I had picked up a copy of *The Tide*, a local newspaper, the previous day. I brought it out from my bag when there was some relative calm to browse through the pages. It was an over ambitious task. A sudden surge in the current of air almost blew the paper from my hands. The pages ruffled noisily as I struggled to fold them. I succeeded but not before the centre spread had flown out of the boat and got buried in the raging wake. I tamely stuffed the rest in my bag as the boat erupted in laughter.

A short distance after Kemebiama, we ran into an ambush. Villagers in about eight canoes and dinghies with cutlasses and axes positioned their boats across the narrow creek in readiness for an attack. A band of local villagers stood by the shore, shouting profanities of all sorts. Apparently, Goddy was prepared for it. I never realized the magnitude of it all until I realized that the parrot woman was lying prostate on the floor by my feet. I had thought it was some cultural ceremony or some communal gathering. Before I knew what was going on, every other passenger was on the floor of the boat. The woman reached for my leg and pulled. It was all the prompting I needed. I dived for safety. It was as much as I could do not to stretch out on the woman. I quickly went for her cage, lifted and pushed it as far as it would go, which was not much. I squeezed myself into the little space created. For a brief moment, I was looking directly into the cage; the fear stricken parrots went into a scuttle before settling down, staring at me directly in the face.

How Samuel managed to hide will forever remain a mystery to me. One moment he was there, by my side, dosing; and the next he was not any longer. When the mayhem finally subsided, he was at the other extreme end of the boat, a distance of about fifteen feet from his seat. Goddy's large body went out of site completely. It was only the sound and movement of the boat that assured the passengers he was still in the skipper's cabin. He dropped from the skipper's seat, and sat on the floor, holding the steering wheel with one hand; and went hard on the throttle, controlling the boat only with his last photo image memory of the waterway.

Sea Truck roared and tore through the barricade of wood and metal like a typhoon. I heard loud bangs and angry voices. I could swear I heard some gun shots, but I was later told it was the sound of metal against the aluminium side panel. "If I survive this I will forever remain immortal," was the thought that went through my mind. There was utter confusion and uncertainty, and missiles of sticks and stones cascaded into the boat, while the angry shouts from the shore provided a baleful background to the pandemonium. A projectile of what must have been loose rock hit the aluminium panel of the skipper's cabin and caromed off in explosive bits across the boat. A few of them ended up on my head. I felt as if needles had been stuck on my head. I did not even have the luxury of rubbing the spot to relieve the excruciating pain. My concern was with the larger threat looming outside the boat. It was the loud reverberation of our boat's engine and the laboured vibration of the aluminium body that assured me of safety and movement away from death.

Soon the bangs stopped, and the angry noise became a distant whine. And suddenly, Goddy's trunk rose from the skipper's cabin, and in his throaty voice announced that danger was over. I heaved a sigh of relief. One after the other, the passengers emerged from their hiding places. To most of them, it was a common experience, but to Samuel and me, it was a close shave with death. Subsequent discussion of the incident was largely in the local language, but with the expressions on their faces and the genuflections, you could judge each contributor's attitude. While some were genuinely infuriated about Goddy's brutality, others saw him as a brave man, who gave the villagers a piece of what they deserved. Bits of the ensuring conversation did filter out.

"*Tank God say dey no get gun,*" a thoroughly frightened man remarked, "*we for don dey tok different ting.*"

"*Gun no fit enter dis boat.*" Goddy remarked, confidently whacking the aluminium panel of the boat with his clenched fist to emphasize his point.

"*If to say we carry our gun, dey no fit…*" It was the skipper's assistant.

"So you carry guns," Samuel asked.

"*How person go dey do dis kind work wey he no go carry gun,*" Goddy continued.

"*Oga na dangerous work,*" a fellow passenger remarked.

"*Dis one way you see na small matter e.*" Goddy went on. "*Some time dey fit carry deadbody come meet you for road say na you kill am. If to say I no comut dere by force, dey fit kill any of us. Dey fit hold dis kopa men, say unless we give dem moni dey no go allow dem go. Na him make dem give us gun say if dey attack us make we dey shoot.*"

"*Hi good now as we don know say dem don give you gun make you kill us,*" an angry passenger, who turned out to be an indigene of a neighbouring village, cut in.

"*How many people I don shoot now? We no dey shoot. I be Izon man myself. How I go dey kill my own people. But when person wan take shop comut your mout or kill you for your korokoro eye. Na hin you go know say to carry gun for dis jungle no be bad ting,*" Goddy concluded.

The reason for the attack by the villages soon became clear from the ensuing discussion: Goddy had destroyed their fishing nets set on the creek on his way to Yenagoa by running over them. What we witnessed was a reprisal. According to some passenger, some villagers deliberately put their nets across the river to foment trouble. Goddy rested his case by claiming he never saw any nets. The journey continued for a long time without any major incident. It was now however evident that he had taken some cue from the nasty experience. Each time we came across fellow travellers, he was more careful, and he even exchanged pleasantries with some.

The ever-present source of worry was the rain, which had increased in intensity. As the boat was moving against the current of air and rain, water was entering the boat, and in no time, we were drenched. Rain pellets bit into our faces and cloths. The roof, a tarpaulin canopy held in place with a metal frame, offered little or no shelter. The loose edges flapped endlessly as the boat rampaged along the creek, adding an eerie background rhythm to the whole misery. Goddy's assistant battled endlessly to keep the tarpaulin in place, while I laboured untiringly trying to move our luggage from the pool of water that had now formed on the floor of the boat. I gave up after several fruitless attempts. Goddy's assistant came periodically to ditch the pool with a plastic hand basin. Also, Goddy helped matters by reducing the speed, thus cutting off the numbing inflow of water, but the misery persisted in the main.

CHAPTER TWO

It was now four o'clock in the evening. We had left Yenagoa around seven o'clock in the morning, and we were told Ukubie was a three-hour ride; but now after nine hours of blistery journey, the familiar dreary refrain was "*Ukubie no far again*".

"*Ukubie no far again! Ukubie no far again! Na hin you dey talk since morning.*" Samuel remarked angrily.

"*My broder, weting I go talk.*" Goddy answered persuasively.

Of course, you probably could not blame anybody, as there was no standard way of measuring distance on the creeks. Travellers on the creeks measure distance by towns and villages strung along the meandering waterway.

The rain, the ever-present tormentor, now became so heavy that you could hardly discern the boundary between the river and the falling water. All efforts at salvaging our luggage from the pool that had formed on the floor of the dinghy were now long abandoned. Some tins of milk that were once in a paper carton scattered loosely in the pool. While some parrots in the cane cage were struggling for dry surface to put their legs, some drank from the pool. A big male duck tied to the opposite aluminium bench also drank happily from the pool, and at some point attempted a swim flutter. The quiver sent a sprinkle of water across the boat, which a gentleman sitting by me took the full brunt of. The boat erupted in laughter. It did not make much of a difference anyway as we were all drenched from the external deluge. The owner pounced on it, tied its wings and legs, and secured it under the bench. I wanted to plead for the poor animal but the energy to do so was not there. I soaked in the joke as I had soaked the ever-present nature's spittle.

"*Na di place way life meet person na him hi dey chop am,*" a passenger remarked.

"*Na true talk. Oga driver, wen you reash clear place I go piss e,*" another passenger said. The boat erupted in laughter.

"*When we reash Ukubie.*" Goddy responded.

"*I beg no carry my own go anywhere, na here I wan chop am e,*" the man countered, and another round of laughter followed.

The trick worked as Goddy reduced speed, steered the boat close to the bank and stopped. The man straightened up and turned, facing away from the boat and did his thing. Two or three other passengers followed his example.

"*When person no fit talk, make hi know say sufferhead done begin,*" the man said as he sat down.

The boat went into another round of hysterics when Goddy, the skipper, came down from the boat to do the same thing.

"*Na so dem dey do am for democracy. When your vote take one pass my own, na you be oga,*" Goddy said, eliciting more hysterics from the passengers. "*Na you be my oga today e!*"

Hunger tugged at my stomach. My last major meal was now twenty-four hours ago. I had three bottles of beer and a plate of steaming *peppersoup* the previous night. Ordinarily, without food, I should nurse the hangover till around noon, but the anxiety of the journey had kept the symptoms at bay so far. The indicators now came in full force. Even Samuel who claimed he was never hungry as long as he had his cigarettes was now complaining of stomach cramp.

The river had become narrower and winding, while the villages appeared much smaller and more forlorn. Goddy manoeuvred

Sea Truck through a dangerously narrow bend. In doing so, he narrowly missed running over a canoe loaded with what looked like tins of palm oil. Characteristically, the paddlers, a woman and a girl, delivered their profanities. The boat took them with philosophical calmness. Even if the boat ran over the canoe, I couldn't care a hoot. I was tired, and sure everybody was.

"Ukubie!" Goddy shouted in the manner of a Lagos bus conductor a short while later.

"Where is it?" I intoned.

The rain had relapsed into an impenetrable thick haze, and you could hardly see beyond your nose. The boat pulled by some monstrous metal mound of a jetty, and Goddy's assistant went into the ceremony of unloading our luggage, which were by then in pieces, from the pool and laying them cautiously on the jetty. Half under water and half above it was a scrappy signpost. At first the portion under water did not make for easy reading because of a refractive distortion. After some effort, it became clear; it was GOVERNMENT SECONDARY SCHOOL, UKUBIE. A feeling of despondency descended over me. "Do human beings live here?" "Is this where I am going to live for one long year?" were questions that tumbled over one another in my mind. The rain, as if in protest against our arrival, became more intense and came down in stinging slings, distorting visibility. Only a handful of wretched looking structures were in sight.

A boy stood in front of what looked like a storehouse talking and pointing in our direction. With our things safely on the jetty, Goddy offered his farewell banter in his characteristic mangled Yoruba. I hardly heard any of it. Talking to him at that point was like talking to a hangman. My eyes were wells of tears mixed with rainwater. Samuel kept quiet. My mind went back to my last day at school.

Flashback!

"Chair! Where have you been?" It was Austin, my roommate.

"Old boy, I have been everywhere."

13

"How was it?"

"Well, Good."

"What was it?"

"What was what?"

"The show now!"

"*You never know? Na two one bo.*"

Austin went into a flight of excitement. He slapped, cuddled and lifted me high as far as the ceiling would allow him.

We had parted in the morning; each headed his department to check his result. It was the end of session. We had finished our examinations some weeks earlier, travelled out for a brief period and were back to school to collect our call-up letters for the National Youth Corps Service.

The previous night, Austin had come back to the room to announce that he made a second-class upper division; his cousin, who was a typist in the departmental office, gave him a hint of his result. But since according to him, and as was obvious from his disposition, both of them were tipsy at the time, he could not rely totally on the information. He got up very early, and left for his department. Austin offered English/Philosophy, while I was in the English/History class. Part of the rumour, according to Austin's cousin, was that two candidates in the English/History class made second-class upper division. I had concluded I could not be one of the two because since his cousin knew me very well, he could as well have told Austin I was one of the two. I got to the department to learn that I was not only one of the two, but was actually on top of the class.

"Old boy, thank God. What must have gone wrong? You know Sylvester actually told me you were not one of the two," Austin said.

"Are you sure he knows his name?" It was Tolu announcing his arrival. I turned to shake hands with him.

"*Bawo ni?* I asked to know his result.

"We did our best," he said.

14

We interpreted that to mean that he made a lower grade. We all tacitly allowed it to rest like that. I later learnt that he was in second-class lower division. Given what we knew about him, it was a good result. Ordinarily, he was a brilliant chap, but he spent most of his time 'mobilizing'- sourcing for money, and therefore did not have much time for his studies.

"Were you at the Student Affairs?" Austin asked.

"I didn't remember that. You know, ever since I checked the result, I have been drifting around campus."

"You are speaking for me." It was Tolu. "I feel some kind of emptiness."

"Emptiness? It is not emptiness: it is what I call success syndrome."

"*Laiwowe.*" Austin interjected.

"*Ayo abara tinntin.* Success is ephemeral. It comes in a flash. As delicate as the butterfly," Peter responded from outside.

Peter and two other friends entered. We exchanged pleasantries and the discussion soon switched to the National Youth Service Corps. We all expressed our preferences regarding posting. Ordinarily, people are posted to areas other than their state of origin.

"Chair I dreamt you were posted to Maidiguri," Tolu taunted me.

"Thank you Mr. Joseph the dreamer. I pray your dream come true. I have always prayed that I am sent to a non-Yoruba-speaking area. I want to know more of the country.

"Why don't you try Okirika?" Austin said. "Or Ogoni, I understand they love foreign flesh." He slapped my hind arm to emphasize his point.

"*Habba*! Nobody does that any longer," Tolu said.

"*Iwo lo mo.* I don't want to be the person to find out. I am not leaving this state, and I have taken care of that. I am the only child of my parents. I am not going to allow any idiot to kill me in the name of some non-existent national unity." This was Peter repeating his well-known position.

15

"I think you are right," Tolu intoned, punctuating the sombre atmosphere created by Peter's submission.

"*Eeemi*! Not with what one has gone through for the past four years. To go and die just like that in one wretched corner of the country." Peter further hammered home his point.

CHAPTER THREE

The reality of my patriotic fancy and commitment stared me cruelly in the face. I felt the warmth of tears welling up in my eyes. Samuel never said anything, but betrayed a lot. He was going through his own version of the tribulation.

"Welcome sir." It was the little boy standing at the door of the zinc structure. He was now on the jetty. I did not know the time he got there.

"Hello!" was all that came out of my mouth.

"Where is the school?" Samuel asked.

"*Hi dey for up.*" He pointed in the direction of the thick forest overlooking the jetty. You could hardly make out any sign of human habitation in the direction he pointed to. He was now attempting to lift Samuel's leather box, but it was too heavy for him to move let alone lift. It did not even occur to me to ask why he was going for our luggage. I gave him a hand, and soon he was moving to the storehouse with the box on his head. Two other boys had joined. They did not talk; they just went for our luggage, each going after what he thought he could carry. I picked up my handbag, but they insisted I should leave it for them.

A flurry of activities was going on in front of the storehouse. A well-dressed gentleman and two women were standing there in the rain. Once in a while, they hollered instructions to the boys carrying our luggage from the jetty. Soon one of the women headed in a sideway direction and disappeared. The remaining man and woman shared an umbrella, and had a spare one. They handed over the two to a girl, who got them and raced in our direction. The umbrellas were meant for us. I did not need an awning at this point. The rain in a strange way gave me some assurance that it was all a dream. Even then using an umbrella at that point was purely academic as we were completely drenched, but we accepted them as a matter of courtesy. The girl handed over the folded one to Samuel, and moved closer to me so that the two of us shared the second one.

"*Sorry e. Rain don beat you,*" the girl said, after sensing the pointlessness of the whole exercise. She collected a few items she could carry in one hand, and we moved in the direction of the storehouse. I was right about the house. The structure was a storehouse built of rough raffia woodwork with zinc roofing and siding. As we later learnt, the construction company that built the secondary school used it as a store for tools and materials. It was given to its present occupier as a token of the company's appreciation of his moral support during the construction of the secondary school. .

When we first entered the house, the impression I got was that the man and his family were taking temporary shelter in the building because of the rain. But as we settled down, we came to realize that it was a full-fledged living quarters. There was not much of a difference between the inside of the house and the exterior in terms of dampness as water dropped from a countless number of spots from the roof to some hand-basin receptacles on the floor, all of which nobody had remembered to empty for some time. There were regular household materials like tables, chairs cupboards etc. Doors and windows were screened with blinds. There were actually three windows, but there were four window blinds, the fourth mock blind marked where the fourth window could have been. A pile of books, a toy telephone box and a turntable music box graced the table-top.

"You are welcome. Come right in. Oh! You are wet! You must be cold!" were the pleasantries with which the gentleman ushered us into his house. They came in torrents, living no room for our response. All we did was move our lips and mumble.

When he finally had a break, I introduced us as National Youth Service Corps members posted to the village. It was a superfluous addendum, for we were in our usual NYSC gear complete with boots and caps. It was in want of something to say. Our host launched into another round of pleasantries: "Oh, we know this! We have been expecting you! You are most welcome to Ukubie town, and to the household of Chief Egypt Benaebi!"etc. He pronounced the word *town* emphatically, and looked directly into my face. I got the message: Ukubie is a town, not a village.

Chief Banaebi's appurtenance stood in sharp contrast to his immediate surroundings. He wore a nice looking navy blue pair of trousers, a sky blue cotton short-sleeve shirt on top of which he wore a sleeveless purple pullover. He had on a horn-rimmed pair of glasses. He seemed to have a grin permanently engrained on his richly dimpled face.

It was getting dark and our host responded by pulling out a Tilley gas lamp and went into the process of putting it on. Initially the exercise produced a ball of fire in the middle of the room to the extent that I was afraid the whole place might go up in flames, but he must have been used to it for he never bothered. He apologized profusely for the embarrassment, which I thought was not necessary, as the bonfire provided us with the much-needed warmth.

In a little while, the gas lamp came on, and the room became so bright that we could see into every corner. It soon became clear that we shared the sitting room with some domestic animals. Some chickens were warming their legs under the crossbar of the table. A nanny goat, apparently disturbed by our presence and the sudden brightness, bolted from a far corner and went into the rain protesting with a grating short sharp cry.

"Oh! Lucy! My wife's goat! It's been raining heavily for the past two weeks. She comes in any time the sleeping place is taken over by water".

We laughed and added our own little repartee. Some young folks appeared at the doorway, and went straight for our luggage. They were boys from the principal's quarters. They must have been fully briefed about our condition for they came with empty containers to carry loose items. We stood up to go with them, but our host would not allow us. His wife, who had disappeared immediately we came in, was preparing something for us. We declined the offer, but he insisted. We agreed and sat down. No sooner had we done so than the principal, Mr. Penane, came in.

"You are here," he said, his face expressionless and barely looking at us directly

"*Yes o!*" I responded.

"How was your journey?"

"*Na wah o!* We managed o."

"What do you expect?" Samuel added in an impertinent manner.

"Sorry eh!"

"If I knew it was going to be like this…." Samuel said, holding his head as if it was going to fall off.

"Don't worry brother. This is a very nice place. You will enjoy it. That is what people say when they first get here," Chief Benaebi intervened.

I kept my cool. It was no use arguing with these people as I had already made up my mind I would go back. Nobody was going to keep me in this wilderness for forty days not to talk of one year. Samuel went into some unfriendly discussion with the principal. I did all I could to calm him, first through pinching, and later through open entreaties. He was really peeved, and he showed it abundantly.

Without doubt, he had every reason to be angry. I never knew Samuel from Adam. I could not even remember seeing him throughout the five weeks we had spent in the orientation camp We met the day I discovered I was posted to Ukubie, and we stuck together ever since as partners in distress. We were saturated with horrible stories about Ukubie. For instance, the name itself, according to some source, meant *a town of lice,* which was intimidating enough to dampen any enthusiasm. It was the remotest part of Rivers State, and it served as a punishment ground for erring civil servants in the state. Recalcitrant civil servants, particularly union activists, were usually posted there to keep them out of circulation. On the account of such stories, we made up our mind we were not going to the place, and set out at effecting a change. It was in the middle of pressing official buttons here and there that Renane, the principal and Samuel met at the secretariat. I was not around then, but when I came back, it was a different Samuel that I met. Penane had worked on him, and given my own earlier predisposition, I was a sitting duck. He passed Penane's pleas and promises to me. We set out from Port Harcourt in good spirit, but the journey from Yenagoa and the little we had seen of the village was enough to break any resolve.

Mrs. Benaebi finally arrived, and we were offered two cups of tea, which we accepted out of sheer courtesy rather than any nutritional appeal.

We finally arrived at the principal's house at about 7.30 pm. To get to his house, we had to traverse a very long slippery ridge on a swampy road. The ridge ran the full span of what used to be a road now completely taken over by water. Benaebi and his wife accompanied us. The entire atmosphere was filled with eerie sounds of frogs, toads and insects. On both sides of the ridge were trenches filled with water, and as we moved along, toads and frogs of different sizes leapt out of the water. We could have been walking in a forest reserve.

"This is our apian way," Benaebi informed us. We all laughed.

Benaebi and his wife discussed with the principal mostly in Ijaw. They only spoke in English any time they got to a subject they thought we should know about. It was actually Benaebi and his wife, who did so, as the principal kept on chirruping like a weaverbird as if we did not exist. The altercation between him and Samuel had created a gap between us. Judging from the accompanying genuflections, their discussion must have centred on either our journey from Yenagoa, or the ridge pathway. I imagined what the trip would have been without the couple.

A short distance from the principal's house, two boys emerged from the dark. They greeted us and engaged the principal in some discussion in Pidgin English. They got kerosene and put on some lamps. They soon withdrew to the background and followed quietly. The subject of their information soon became clear as we sighted the principal's quarters in the distance. It was brightly lit, as we soon found out, with gas lamps, the type we had seen in Benaebi's place.

Two women and some children stood on the veranda to receive us. They were the principal's wives and children. We exchanged greetings, and they disappeared into the inner rooms. The procession entered the house, and settled in the sitting room.

The principal's house was a four- bedroom bungalow - a prefabricated type, complete with all the modern conveniences - electric fittings and water points- except that there was no electricity, and the taps never ran. Whoever designed and constructed the building never had its present occupants in mind. Everything was where and how it should not be. The furnishing was Spartan and disorganised. The doors and windows were not screened and most of the glass louver blades were missing. The living room was littered with all sorts of incongruous items: rain-boots, plastic containers, outboard engine petrol tanks etc. There was no decoration of any sort, except a picture of the principal in academic gown, which hung on the wall as if put there in a hurry. Two dining chairs stood by the dining table, while the rest, three or four, in a broken heap by the corner, looked invitingly at their surviving colleagues by the table. A trophy with a missing handle stood submissively in company of some utensils on the table.

Benaebi remained the only bright spot. He provided the fun and commentary. He introduced the principal's house as the white house to which we all laughed. His wives, too, were first ladies. When Samuel reminded him that two cannot be first, he replied that there was a tie, and therefore the second slot was still vacant. We had a meal of *gaari* and fish stew, and soon we bid everybody good night and retired to a room where the contents of our thoroughly drenched luggage were neatly laid out to dry. We reviewed the trip and our ordeal. It became clear to me that Samuel was not too keen about going back, so I resolved to keep whatever plan I had to my chest. I soon drifted into a sound and dreamless sleep.

I woke up the following morning feeling strangely refreshed. I first opened my eyes around 4.30 am when a rooster directly behind the room sounded its wake up call. And thereafter, I found it difficult to go back sleep. Samuel was by my side snoring happily. The previous night, I had advised him against taking sleeping pills, but judging from the soundness of his sleep, I was not sure he heeded my advice. I laid there staring into space. My mind raced through the possible misfortune that lied in wait for me in my new dwelling. I began to think up all kinds of excuses and plans to leave Ukubie. I would wake up in the morning complaining of diarrhoea. I had some purgative tablets. An overdose would do the trick: visit the toilet several times, and to the knowledge of the principal; refuse to take any meal. I was allergic to the environment. The principal would send me packing unless he wanted a dead body on his hands. No! That option was too craven. Walk up to the principal, and tell him point blank I was going back to Port Harcourt for reposting. No! Too daring! I finally made up my mind on the first option. I soon drifted into another light sleep in which I dreamt, and saw Goddy. However, in my dream, he was not a boat skipper but a preacher. He was trying, without success, to gain the attention of a riotous congregation. I was making jest of his large cassock and ungraceful movements when Samuel stirred me up.

23

"You can't sleep all day"

"Haa! Good morning," I said, yawning.

"Morning. Your principal has been here"

"I see. What does he want?"

"*To greet you, now.* The bathroom is out there, and he says your meal is ready"

I rolled over expecting to feel pains and aches, but strangely, I did not feel any soreness. I stood up to catch a glimpse of Ukubie through the window, and I had another surprise. The spectacle was not as horrifying as I had expected. In the distance were two other bungalows similar to, but not as large as, the one we were in. Facing the two was a block of rooms. I guessed it was the administrative building. But beyond these structures was a wretched looking house. It was too close to the block of rooms and the bungalows not to be part of a common whole. As we learnt later, it was the community's addition to the structures put in place by the government. Ironically, the only sign of life came from the house. A man and a woman stood in front. The woman was stoking a fire, while the man fumbled with some mass of tangled lines. Beyond these structures was a thick evergreen forest.

I turned to see Samuel fumbling with a stick of cigarette and a box of matches: time for the morning smoke. I advised that we move out of the room to the veranda.

The veranda provided a good and total picture of Government Secondary School Ukubie. All the structures, except one, were of equal standard with the principal's house. It consisted of two blocks of classrooms, an office block, a laboratory, two blocks of hostels and three bungalows as staff quarters. The entire grounds floated on water. Pathways were ridges similar to the one that brought us to the compound the previous night. The place looked deserted. This was expected as the students were on holiday. A few locals traversed the compound, apparently to get to their farms.

The principal soon joined us, and we exchanged greetings. The wives too, having overheard us, came out to greet us. A third woman whom we did not see the previous night also came out with them. She was introduced as Kehinde, the principal's cousin. When I heard the name, a Yoruba name, I was prompted to speak to her in Yoruba to which she only grinned. The principal explained that not only was she not Yoruba, but also that she did not speak a word of Yoruba.

"Please, what will you like for breakfast?" The principal asked.

"Anything", Samuel answered.

"Can we have bread?" I asked.

"Bread!" the principal exclaimed with a wry smile. He did not need to go further. He was telling us that we could not get bread in Ukubie.

"Next time I travel, I will bring bread from Port Harcourt." You can't eat Ukubie bread.

"How about boiled yam?"

"Well, it's OK." I said.

Soon we had a breakfast of yam and fish *peppersoup*. It was incredible how such a meal could come from the principal's household. We temporarily forgot our travails. A few visitors, members of staff and some villagers came in, apparently to see us. News of our arrival had circulated in the village and a few villagers and friends of the school came in to see for themselves.

Among the callers was the village Chief, who also doubled as the village school headmaster. The principal introduced us lavishly. His emphasis was on me. The reason for this soon became clear to me. I was the first university graduate English teacher Government Secondary ever had. Chief Benaebi came in at this point and resumed his commentator duty. He introduced and provided the background to each visitor. The village chief/headmaster expressed his happiness and promised us a nice time in Ukubie. Being put on a pedestal at this point was not good for my plan. Even though I was inwardly impressed by the hospitality being showered on us, I tried to maintain an outward look of unfriendliness and despondency.

CHAPTER FOUR

I did make good my intention to leave Ukubie. As the days wore on my resolve to go back to Port Harcourt for re-posting grew stronger. Each day brought its attendant repulsive revelation about the environment. On the third day of our arrival, for example, I wrote a series of letters to friends and family—only to learn, that Ukubie had no postal agency!

The opportunity to leave came on a platter of gold. Benaebi breezed in on a fine morning to inform us that he would be travelling to Yenagoa on a business trip. He was going in a chartered boat. I did not allow the opportunity to slip. I told the principal that I was going to Port Harcourt to get some supplies, particularly drugs, and to see a doctor. I was pleasantly astonished when he suggested a hospital in Port-Harcourt to me. He explained to me that the Ukubie community depended on a hospital boat, which in good times came to Ukubie twice a year. We were in the month of September, and the boat was yet to make its first visit. I packed a few items of my belongings, and left Ukubie.

I landed in Port-Harcourt to the warm embrace of friends. After listening to my tales of woe, they all rallied round to assist me in my bid to effect a change of posting. Nothing we did worked: it was a shuffle in the swamp. Soon I became a notorious character in the secretariat. I was almost always the first and the last person in the building. On a few occasions I slept in the premises in company of other corps members with similar problems. After two weeks of unsuccessful lobbying, I decided to give up everything about youth service, and left for Lagos.

I was in Lagos for upward of three weeks. I tried as much as possible to blot Ukubie out of my consciousness, but the more I tried the more it kept coming both in my dreams and in real situations. Each time I came across a friend or any acquaintance I needed to explain my presence in Lagos. Soon I got tired of the exercise, and I began to have a change of heart.

Events took a dramatic turn one evening when an old relation, who was paying my uncle a visit, asked me whether there were human beings at Ukubie, and insinuated that I was a coward. I took her comment in bad faith, and openly branded her a witch and an enemy of my mother. She tactically apologized, and we allowed the matter to rest like that. On a deeper reflection, I concluded she was right. I walked up to her the following day, thanked her, and told my uncle I was ready to go back and make the best of Ukubie. It was a big relief to my uncle, who had secretly expressed concern about my action. The following day he came home with an air ticket and all kinds of imaginable supplies and provisions. He even toyed with the idea of buying a small power generator, which I thought was unnecessary. The following day I set out on my second trip to Ukubie.

I arrived at Ukubie on a sunny afternoon. It was one of those days that Mother Nature smiled on Ukubie and allowed sunshine to reach down. I could see the entire village in a fine perspective. There was not much difference from my earlier impression; it was an assemblage of huts and a few houses. The school had resumed, and had just closed for the day, and students were streaming out from the ridge path that led to the school compound. Their white-upon-blue uniform added some brightness to the otherwise dull deep green of the forest background. As they passed by, they looked in the direction of the jetty and its visitor, *Ayakpor*, the boat that brought me, but since it was the boat's return trip, during which it did not carry any goods, they showed no interest in it. And since I was not in my NYSC uniform, there was no way they could recognize me as their Youth Corp teacher. But my bearing and disposition must have set me apart from the crowd, for before long a group came, four boys and two girls. They must have suspected I was the second Youth Corps teacher. They approached me for confirmation, and brightened up when I told them I was. They scrambled for my luggage, each struggling to lay hands on at least a piece. The two girls, who had nothing to carry after the boys had outsmarted them, practically snatched my handbag, which I strung over my shoulder, and my umbrella from me.

"You are welcome sir." "How was your journey?" "We have been expecting you." They greeted me with grand gesture. Other students stopped to catch a glimpse of this new centre of attention. In no time, I was surrounded by an excited group of students. Even others who did not stop looked in my direction with excitement. Just as they were telling me of Samuel's whereabouts, he appeared in the distance and shouted as soon as he saw me, breaking into a run. We collided in a huge hug .He was extremely delighted to see me.

"You are back?"

"Yes, I am here."

"Thank you! Thank God."

It was obvious from the level of excitement demonstrated by Samuel that he never expected me back. In fact, I never gave him reason to expect me. I had indirectly asked him to help me bring the things I left behind to Port Harcourt, and even told him where to deposit them. He must have judged from the volume of my luggage, a suitcase and two fat cardboard cartons containing supplies and provision that I had come to stay.

"Old boy you are really prepared for this jungle," he remarked, looking at the two cartons.

"Well, having been here once. I don't have to be told of what to expect."

I was surprised that the students carrying my things did not move in the direction of the school compound, instead they headed in the direction of the village.

"*Oga don drive me comut for compound o!*"

Samuel explained that shortly after I left, the principal moved him to a house by the end of the village. We stopped at Chief Benaebi's house. He was not at home. I greeted members of his household, which now included an old man, who I later learnt was his father. We then moved in the direction of the village.

Soon we arrived at a house near what looked like a school premises. It was a bungalow built in the fashion of the houses we saw on our way across the village. The structure had seen better days. The paint had faded off. The cement plaster had peeled off in several spots exposing the mud and inner woodwork. The building was crowded by two untended giant almond trees, which gave it a chilly and damp ambience. The interior was not different; the ceiling had telltale dark perches of roof leakages, termites had been given a free hand, and they were doing a great job on the window and doorframes. Louver blades were either not there or at best replaced with plywood or cardboard substitutes. It was a three-bedroom piece. The kitchen was directly behind the house, separated with an unpaved and slippery ground, but Samuel had converted the third room to a kitchen. The building was originally intended as the living quarters for the primary school's headmaster, but since the current headmaster was also the Chief of the village and lived in his private house, the house was transferred to the new secondary school. I took in these details without any displeasure.

I did not allow this initial disappointment to dampen my newfound enthusiasm. I knew within me it was a problem that could be solved. The students deposited my luggage, and I gave them a carton of Cabin biscuits, which they accepted with courteous reluctance.

It was not difficult for me to see the kind of despair Samuel had been going through and I felt responsible for this in a way. If I had stayed all along, we would have presented a joint and stronger opposition against the decision to put us in this miserable environment. I now saw him as a blood brother and somehow inwardly felt remorse for my action.

We spent the next hour or so reviewing our individual activities since we parted. I went over my unsuccessful attempt at Port Harcourt to effect a change of posting, and my adventure to Lagos. He was astonished to learn how far and daring I went. He also told me about his travails. The principal moved him to the present abode the second day I left against his protestations. His major problem had been loneliness, and the insect-infested abode. He did not need to tell me about the insects, for I could see from the telltale rashes all over his body. The disorder in the sitting room was a photocopy of the rough existence he had been going through. Bottles, cigarette butts and utensils littered the floor. As soon as we entered, he went into the rituals of cleaning and rearranging the room.

"*Na wah o*! You have been living swell," I exclaimed.

"*Wetin man go do*."

Shortly after we settled down, a man by the name Benedict came in. He was so light in complexion that one could mistake him for an albino. He was slightly bald and exuded calm and amiability. He was the site technician for WACO, a construction company that was to build a health centre for Koloama District for which Ukubie is the headquarters. He had been in Ukubie for the previous two years and the construction was yet to commence. As we later learnt, he was put on the ground as window-dressing to convince any supervising government official that the company was alive and active. Samuel must have told him about me because he mentioned my name offhand .He greeted me profusely, and congratulated Samuel.

"Welcome to the city," he said, laying the usual undue emphasis on the word city.

"Thank you."

A short while after, an elderly man, a member of staff, came in to give Samuel a balm for his rashes. He was on his way to his farm. He was delighted to see me. Samuel introduced him as Chief Abraham, and asked him if he would bring snails from the farm.

"That would be tomorrow morning. I set the traps in the evening, and go there to collect very early in the morning," he explained.

"You set traps for snails?" I asked.

"Yes."

"How?"

"Oh, you have just come. You will know before you leave Ukubie. Were it not that you have just come, I would have asked you to follow me," he replied with some air of authority.

"I was surprised the first time I heard it myself," Benedict added.

"I can't believe it," I said.

"I will convert you," Chief Abraham boasted.

After our guests left, Samuel showed me my room. He brought my things he had kept in his room, and I stacked them in a corner, together with the new lot. Somebody had done a very good job of cleaning the room. I suggested a visit to the principal, but Samuel told me he had travelled to Port Harcourt. However a walk to the school compound, which was located at the other extreme of the village, was not a bad idea.

The stroll offered me the first clear view of the village. Even though we had taken the same route when I arrived, the details never came to me the way they did the second time.

Ukubie is a very small village located on the Akpoi creek. It was made up of about two hundred houses, counting every structure. The settlement was situated exclusively on one side of the river. Not even a shed or garden strayed across the river. You could almost conclude it was a taboo to carry out any activity on the other side. It was a thick and dense evergreen forest, with impenetrable undergrowth.

There was only one road, if you could call it so. It was largely the coalescence of opening spaces in front of houses that formed the alleyway, and it cut the village into two unequal halves. There was actually no need for a road as there were no vehicles or even bicycles. There was only one bicycle in the village, as I later learnt, which came down once in a year in December when the rains withdrew a little to give it some dry ground on which it could ride. The remaining part of the year it spends in the ceiling rafters. The halve adjourning the river was the smaller of the two, and since the life of the community centred on the river; it was the livelier of the two. The other half had more houses and huts, but largely unplanned. You got around by snaking your way through spaces between houses and verandas. The houses were mostly small bungalows built of mud supported with raffia woodwork. Most houses had no front doors, and when I made the observation, Benedict simply said, "Because there are no thieves."

The road was the playground for the community. It was evening time, so children and adults alike flooded it. Women and old men sat in front of their houses to catch a glimpse of whatever was going on. Some nursing mothers too, mostly top bare, sat in front of their houses with their children strung on their laps, sucking from exposed breasts.

Even if we had set out for a public introduction to the village, it couldn't have been better arranged. Members of staff, students, and some interested villagers greeted us. And expectedly, since most of them were seeing me for the first time I was the focus of attention. We finally arrived at the other extreme end, the jetty side. We tarried to observe some heavily-laden canoe discharging its cargo. It was the eve of the market day, and traders were already arriving.

Chief Benaebi came out of his house with a shout when he saw me.

"Who is this?" he shouted.

"Chief!"

"So you are back?"

"I called here in the afternoon."

"Is that right? Oh! I went to the village meeting."

"Village?" I asked sarcastically.

"Sorry, City!" We all laughed. The wife came out from the direction of the village. We exchanged greetings, and she retired into the storehouse.

"Thanks for the other time."

"No! What did I do?"

"I appreciate it," I insisted.

"Please don't mention it."

"How are the twins?"

"Fine,"

"And Lucy!" — *a goat*

"Oh! Right there!" he said, pointing at the goat feeding happily on some item around the corner of his house.

"You must be happy now." he said, turning to Samuel.

"Thank you sir," Samuel said, beaming with a smile.

We told him we were going to the school compound. He informed us in turn that the vice principal had just left his place. It was the first time I would learn that the school had a vice principal. He arrived after I had left. Chief Benaebi joined us and we strolled to the school compound. Our first port of call was the principal's quarters. The household was very happy to see me. We greeted them and left for the vice principal's house, which was one of the other two bungalows.

He was glad to see us, and he demonstrated it to the extreme. Mr Tamuno was a University of Ibadan graduate. He treated us to a sumptuous super of *gaari* and fish *peppersoup*. We spent the remaining part of the evening there. After the meal, he brought out assorted drinks: beer, whisky and brandy. Our topics of general discussion ranged from the village to politics. It did not take me long to discover that he was as disgruntled about his presence in Ukubie as we were.

33

His dissatisfaction was mixed with a tinge of happiness, because he was also promoted vice principal, but he also believed that he could have been happier as a vice principal elsewhere. By the time we left his house it was pitch dark. Chief Benaebi and Benedict saw us to our house. Samuel and I talked for a little while before each of us retired to our different rooms for the night.

CHAPTER FIVE

Life in Ukubie was very boring, as expected. We woke up each morning, had our bath, took our breakfast, and went to school. By two o' clock in the afternoon, the school was over; we retired to our house, and had our lunch. We spent the rest of the day reading or sleeping. Chief Benaebi and Benedict were our main companions. Soon age and individual differences separated us into two. I gravitated towards Benaebi while Samuel moved towards Benedict and a few grown-up students. Even though Benedict was of the same age with me, he found more things in common with Samuel. We had other common friends, but none of them moved as close to us as Benaebi and Benedict.

It soon dawned on me that if I was to make the best out of my stay in Ukubie, I would have to be inventive, and not only find a way of keeping myself busy, but also find a way of inviting people to our house to keep our company. First, we needed to know the goings-on in the outside world. None of us had a radio, and in the entire Koloama District, it was anathema to think of newspapers. Even in Yenagoa, the headquarters of the entire division, newspapers and magazines were rare commodities. Of course travelling was out of consideration. The only transport boat was *Ayakpor*, which came to Ukubie once in two weeks. Its journey from Yenagoa to Ukubie normally took two days. We learnt that our trip with Sea Truck was a rare luck, and of course throughout our stay, we never saw the boat again or anything like it.

I was amazed at the level of ignorance or lack of interest in the outside world displayed by the school teachers. Their lives revolved around the school, their farms and the river on which they carried out fishing just like other villagers.

I learnt from some source that the school had a bush radio. According to the source, the radio came with a consignment of laboratory equipment a few years back, but ever since it had disappeared, and nobody was sure of its whereabouts. This was long before the present principal came. When I mentioned it to him, he was as blank as every other person, but he promised to go into the matter.

Things started happening when I mentioned it to Chief Benaebi. Even though he was not a member of staff, he gave me every detail about the history of the radio - how it came to the school, its first user and its present custodian. By the third day, the principal walked into our house with the set blaring music from the test transmission of a rogue FM station from a neighbouring state. I later leant that Benaebi personally went to the custodian, an administrative assistant, and alerted him trouble was heading his way. The radio was found in a conspicuous corner of the school laboratory the following day.

The radio dramatically transformed our social life. It was always with us, both at home and at school. It was a 1965 Philips set with medium and long wave bands. It was our window on the world, and as it turned out, the source of information for the school community. At any given period of the day, you could predict what station the radio would be. Very early in the morning we listened to some local stations, like Ondo Radio Corporation, Ogun State Broadcasting Station, Radio Kaduna and Radio O.Y.O. Between 7:00 and 8:00 a.m., we shuffle between Radio Nigeria and some international stations like the BBC and VOA,

The rogue FM station from a neighbouring state entertained us with music in the afternoons and evenings.

We came to school each morning with the latest news of happenings in the outside world, and discussed them during breaks and free periods. It usually started with general briefing of the news items, followed by comments and general discussion. A few developed interests, especially one Mr Teneni. He was always anxious to know the development on the political scene, particularly when the political parties were being formed in 1979. But others couldn't care less. There was Mr Tebiowei, for example, whose comment was almost always, *"Wetin you want take dis tin do".* Or *"Na hin we go shop?"* Or *"You no sabi dis man,* he is a politician."

There was 'Rev' Amadala, an extremely impassive individual. He taught Religious Studies and History in the lower classes. His perception of discussion is speech-making. He would wait for an opportune time in any discussion, usually a long break between speakers, stand up and clear his throat to call for attention and introduce his speech, invariably, with either "I think we are not addressing the real issue," or "Gentlemen and ladies in *absinthial.*" Of course, this was always followed with shouts of "A-m-a-d-a-l-a!" The h-o-n-o-r-a-b-le Reverend!" His contribution was always the *Nunc Dimittis* to any free discussion, because by the time he finished, half of the discussants would have left, and the few remaining must have been so thoroughly bugged down by the share woolliness of his argument that reacting to his point of view would be impossible or simply superfluous.

I used to play draughts at school, so my next initiative was to construct a draughts board. To accomplish this task, we needed a flat wooden sheet. I found an old plywood sheet from the school store, and from this we were able to construct the board and the seeds, A few developed interests, especially the younger folks. Chief Abraham helped out with the painting. Soon staff players converged in our house after school hours and weekends. At times, we played far into the night, using candles and lanterns. It attracted players and spectators alike, and with it, we were able to keep boredom at bay.

It took me only a short while to know that the principal had some measure of respect for me. He did not extend the same deference to my colleague. He was always eager to listen to my point of view. Even, on issues that had nothing to do with our welfare, he asked for my opinion. With this realization, I had to revise my unfriendly posture, which had been largely influenced by his role in getting us to Ukubie; after all he was protecting the interest of his school.

One afternoon, I approached him to request some sporting equipment. We had actually approached the games-master for volleyball materials about a week earlier, but he had told us point-blank that it was beyond his powers to do such a thing. When I asked him to pass our request to the principal, he recommended that we should talk to him directly. Mr Tarila had called in our office the afternoon to ask about the outcome of our request from the principal. When we told him we had not approached him, he advised that one of us went to him. I stood up and headed for the principal's office, two rooms away.

"Good afternoon sir."

"Chief Olo-runto-ba. Good afternoon. Did I get it right?" He had problem pronouncing my last name.

"Oh! Perfect," I said, even though it was the worst attempt he had ever made in getting my name right. I didn't consider a disputation on phonetics relevant at that particular moment.

"Please sit down. How are you today," he said, looking at me expectantly.

"I am all right," I replied.

"I have even wanted to see you. Please sit down," he insisted. With that I pulled one of the chairs in front of his table, and sat down.

"Well, which comes first?" he asked. "Since you made the move, I think you should come first," he added before I could say anything. He was all the while standing, involuntarily arranging files and papers on his table as if he was making room for whatever I intended to drop on the table.

"Not a serious matter, really. I was going to ask if you could be so kind as to give us volleyball materials. We have already prepared a court just behind the laboratory there," pointing in the direction of the laboratory block.

He covered his face with his palms, and when he removed his hands, he revealed the brightest Penane I had ever seen. He was all smiles. I was confused.

"What a coincidence. You know I just ..., ok. You will have your ball, but I was just going to ask you if you could assist Mr Tarila as the assistant games master. You can see that no sporting activities have been going on since you came. We have been like that for the past two years. He is supposed to be an expert in Physical Education, but I haven't seen the effect. Please, anything you can do."

He did not give me any room to accept or decline. All I had time to say was: "All right." Before I knew it, he was up, he brought out a heavy bunch of keys from one of the drawers of his table, and led me out of the office to the store where he showed me an array of sporting equipment: tennis rackets, balls and nets, footballs and jerseys, hockey sticks, etc, etc. We rummaged through the pile, and finally found four volleyballs out of which I took two along with a net and a manual pump. Just as we were about to leave the store, I saw a pile of window blinds in a corner of the store. When I asked what they were kept there for, he asked whether we needed them. I said yes and he asked me to take some.

"By the way, how is your quarters down there?"

"You mean our den?" I said, stretching out my arm, still spotted with signs of mosquito's bites of the previous night.

"Would you like staying within the school premises?" he asked casually.

I could not believe my ears.

"What did you say?" I asked.

It was not that I did not hear what he said, but the response was to allow me think up a proper way to react to the issue he had just touched on. I had learnt that the third of the three bungalows within the school premises was vacant. It had never been occupied since its completion some five years earlier. The principal never considered any of his staff worthy of occupying it. You really could not blame him. Many of them were grade two teachers, and their life-style was largely rural and definitely not compatible with such modern structures. They prepared their meals with firewood just like the local farmers and fishermen, and since the buildings were the prefabricated wooden type, it could mean putting the houses in unnecessary risk. All these facts I learnt through my ever-reliable grapevine, Chief Benaebi.

"I mean moving to the compound," he further said.

"Yes! Yes! We have been having a lot of problems... actually. Mosquitoes and termites, you know ...," I babbled.

"Well, I think you can move to the house by the vice principal's place. The house is good and clean. It has never been occupied really," he pronounced.

"Thanks. God bless you."

"You can come for the keys after school hours.... Or, why don't we do it this way. I'll get some students to clean the place; you can collect the keys after."

"That's alright. Thanks."

With that I left for an afternoon Literature in English class. My students could not have failed to notice the excitement I exuded. I walked around the classroom with a new bounce. The achievements were too much for one day!

I had particularly boasted to Chief Benaebi that I would secure the use of the apartment, and lo and behold, there it came on a platter of gold. He had asked me to forget the idea because the principal had told him he would never give the place out to anybody. It would also confirm Samuel's claim that the principal had a soft spot for me. It was one of my happiest days in Ukubie.

I reclined royally on my office table as I reeled out my achievements of the afternoon to Samson and Mr Tarila. They had dispersed earlier on, and left for their respective classes after waiting for me for some time. They had just come back after school hours to know the outcome. It was more than Samuel could take. Tarila stood looking at me, his face expressionless. I held back the assistant games master's angle, since I didn't know how he would take it. Let him get it from the horse's mouth.

"*Oloruntoba today no be April fool now!*" Samuel interjected.

"You think I am lying?"

"Why will he be lying?" Tarila said in his usual cool manner.

"Not really. But----," He stammered and looked in the direction of the volley balls, the pump, the net and the window blinds lying in a heap on his table, his face a canvass of exhilaration and perplexity.

"May be this one will convince you: Tomorrow, we move into the school premises," I said and pointed in the direction of our new home.

"Can we go home? It's past three o'clock!" Samuel concurred in exasperation, and stood up picking his things from the top of his table

Just as we were leaving the office, the principal came in company of some students. Characteristically, he just called my attention, pointed in the direction of the students, and left. I picked up the pantomime from where he left, explained his gestures, and together we herded the students towards our new home.

This was the clarification everybody needed to believe me. Samuel suddenly became overtly exited. Tarila too, having been caught up in the excitement of the whole drama could not leave. He joined us in the cleaning of the house. He therefore became our first guest, and without telling him, we gave him the honour and respect to our last day in Ukubie.

We decided to move the following day, and since that day was going to be our last day in the village, we decided to have an impromptu party. We invited our immediate friends and had a bash.

CHAPTER SIX

Chief Benaebi was not an indigene of Ukubie. His hometown was a village, half a day away from Ukubie. He sold outboard engines and spare parts. His office and shop was a shed by the market place. He took his time decorating it, making it look like an executive office with cheap office equipment he inherited from an old business partner. He even had a toy telephone box conspicuously displayed on the table. Stories had it that he bamboozled his illiterate customers by telling them that he would make contact with the phone to order their products.

Chief Benaebi was a prime example of the difference between reality and appearance. Outwardly, he had the appurtenance of a university professor or a business executive whereas he was no more than an emancipated village boy trying to make ends meet. He had the language and carriage to match. The village knew him as Businessman, and he was generally popular with the younger folks, while the older folks treated him with caution and masked contempt. His abode was the store of the construction company that built the school which, according to him, was given to him in appreciation of the assistance he gave to the company. He had wanted to put up his own personal house but as a matter of policy, he said, non-indigenes were not allowed to put up structures in Ukubie.

He was a close friend of the principal, and for this, he had a strong relationship with the school, and even taught Literature in the lower classes. The students respected or feared him just as any other teacher, and he was generally treated as a member of staff. What he did not know about Ukubie was not worth knowing. He had information about everybody, and would reel out such at the slightest prompting. He usually started by "so you don't know this" or "lend me your ears", and would continue from there, providing every detail about the personality or issue involved. He was very entertaining, and you never had any dull moment with him.

I spent most of my free moments with Benaebi in his 'executive office'. One bright afternoon, after school hours, I called at his office just to ask after his well-being. Soon after I arrived, a customer called for some spare parts. After the usual transaction, the man asked why he had stayed away from their village and reminded him of the annual football match. Benaebi's reaction was electrifying.

"Amoo!Amoo! Amoo!" he grabbed his head with both hands, jumping hysterically in his chair.

"You mean you don forget?" the customer said, looking askance. *I tink say na you be di chairman for dis year.*

"I forgot c-o-m-p-l-e-t-e-l-y!" he exclaimed.

"I don remind you now," the customer said.

"Obe to dun, we are going to Akpoi this afternoon."

"What!" I said, looking totally lost.

"Oh! I have not introduced my friend to you. This is Mr Oloruntoba, *Obe to dun* -the only Yoruba expression he knew and called me jokingly- a Youth Corper here. He will be there with me. This is Mr Kimse the Secretary of Akpoi town, just a stone throw from here."

"Good afternoon," I shook hands with the man, still unsure of what the excitement was all about.

Soon, Kimse left and Benaebi explained to me that he got an invitation to a football match taking place in a nearby village that afternoon, but had completely forgotten. As he was talking, he dug into a side drawer of his table and pulled out a hand written invitation card, which he passed on to me to read. It was my turn to have my laugh—and a deep one indeed. I burst into an uncontrollable fit of laughter.

"Chief o!" I finally managed to say.

"Oh I am serious," he said, wondering why I was sceptical.

"Who says you are not! Football match! Jesus! In this deciduous forest!" I managed to say between hysterics.

"And where is this soccer village."

"Oh! Just around the bend"

"On the same river?"

"You mean you don't know Akpoi."

"I have no idea there is any village along this creek big enough to hold a football field, not to talk of a match."

The idea of anybody playing football in and around Ukubie did not only sound funny to me but stupid. If anybody expected a game to be played in Ukubie, it should not be football, because the whole area was not only swampy, it was practically under water all the year round. For instance, the school premises were waterlogged to the extent that almost everybody wore rain boots to get around. It was the same thing in and around the village. The school could not even think of constructing a football field in spite of the fact that the school had an abundant supply of the necessary equipment for the game, boots, jerseys, etc.. It just did not make any sense.

"Just go and prepare. I will go for the principal," he said, after seeing the futility of trying to convince me. Well, since I had nothing doing, I thought it was a way of whiling away time. I went home and informed Samuel about it. The idea equally sounded implausible to him, but since I sounded somehow convincing to him, he dressed up, and we hurried down to join Benaebi and the vice-principal, who were already waiting. I was surprised to find out that the vice-principal was also enthusiastic about the idea. We were told the principal could not make it because of some domestic matter.

We set out in a dingy fixed with an outboard engine. Naturally, Benaebi was the operator. He turned out in traditional attire, which gave him an awkward but regal look. He insisted on teaching me how to handle the boat, which I accepted. I had already started taking lessons a couple of weeks earlier. After a few false starts, I got the hang of it, and was able to pilot the boat, even though at a very slow pace. We proceeded very slowly, coming to a total stop each time we came across a canoe. The reason for asking me to handle the boat soon became clear to me: Chief Benaebi as the chairman wanted to complement his regal appearance with being driven. This soon became clear to me the way he waved to passers-by, whether they greeted him or not. As soon as he discovered that I was doing well enough, he positioned himself royally on the cross bench next to me, while Samuel and the vice-principal sat on the front bench.

Under one hour, we came to a group of huts by the creek, and Chief Benaebi announced that we were in Akpoi. Samuel and I exchanged knowing glances.

"Is this the place?" Samuel asked superfluously.

"Oh yes," Benaebi said, coming to take over the control of the boat so as to dock it properly.

Just as we were disembarking, and still wondering what the drama was all about, two men emerged from one of the huts and welcomed us. One took over the boat, and the other led us along a path beside one of the huts. The path led to a large opening surrounded by more huts. More people, men and women, came out to greet us, and from the enthusiasm and warmth they exuded, it was obvious something great was in the offing. But still the idea of this village and football match appeared utterly incongruous to me. We were led into a structure bigger than the surrounding huts, which we understood was the house of the village chief. The household was in a festive mood. Children scuttled around noisily, and women moved about with cooking materials and condiments. We settled down, and Benaebi introduced us lavishly. The chief, in a loin cloth, was utterly delighted, thanking us profusely for coming as he moved from one person to another shaking hand.

When Benaebi mentioned I was Yoruba, he threw up his arms in excitement and hollered to somebody. A young lady came in.

"Iyawo! *Na your people be dis e!*" he said to the woman.

"*E nle o(hello),*" I said to the woman, forcing a smile.

The young lady looked blankly at me. She looked beautiful, but the harsh environment seemed to have left its mark on her. She was not actually Yoruba, Benaebi explained to me, it was just that she was given a Yoruba name because the chief, the father, was a 'Yorubaphile'. When I told them that *Iyawo* was the Yoruba word for *wife*, they did not believe me, and were not only terribly disappointed, but were almost convinced that I was not Yoruba myself. As Benaebi revealed to me later, the Chief said I was counterfeit Yoruba. To him, *Iyawo* meant a beautiful woman. The woman too did not like it, as her countenance changed immediately, and she left the room unceremoniously.

A man of about sixty, accompanied by Kimse, emerged at the door, and with the old man came the first sign of football. It was as much as I could do not to laugh, and that included looking away from Samuel and the vice-principal, who were also suppressing their own emotional outburst. He wore a pair of what looked like soccer boots. They were soccer boots all right, judging from the traditional stripes across the insteps, but besides, they were collections of pieces of leather strung together with twine and flexible wire. Some length of crepe bandage and rags formed the hose. The Chief introduced him as Okoko Abednego, the captain of the town team. It was an opportunity to release tension, as we all burst into laughter.

The whole picture gradually became clear. The football match was an annual event for the Akpoi village. It was always between the village eleven and the local primary school eleven. The idea started when the former headmaster, an ex-footballer, came back to the village as the first teacher of the primary school. The story had it that he single-handedly fought for the establishment of the elementary school. He used to invite young men of the village to play football with his pupils. When he died in a boat mishap some years back, a football match between the village folks and the primary school was organised in his memory, and the practice had endured ever since. It was actually a remembrance day for the late headmaster, and the whole village prepared for it with gusto.

In next to no time, drums were rolled out, and villagers, men and women, started arriving. Everybody, including women, appeared in one sporting dress or another. There were shirts and knickers of different shades. The cynosure of all eyes was an old woman of about sixty years, who came out in khaki shorts and a T-shirt, emblazoned with the logo of the Dallas Cowboys, topped with a fez cap. She had a whistle, which she blew in time to the cadence of the drumming. The whole gathering roared in laughter when she came in, and in response she did some faltering steps, and the crowd went mad.

It was all the entire gathering needed to get into full swing. Soon a dancing circle materialised around the drummers, and the whole arena was soaked in a verdant of singing and dancing. The women dictated the thrust and pace. They would do a few forward steps, during which they waved their handkerchiefs, and suddenly stop, bend the upper parts of their bodies, and shake their bosoms to the rhythm. It was thrilling. There were many songs, but the most popular of them all was the one initiated by the old woman:

My mama no giri me e,
Sikiri sikiri me e,
My mama no giri me e,
Oh baby dey go
Asawo.
:
(My mother would not allow me.
Secretly watching over me.
My mother would not allow me
There goes the baby!
Prostitute)

It ignited the atmosphere, and sent the dance circle into frenzy. Before we knew it, we were in the circle, drafted by the same old woman, who now assumed the role of a compeer. She went round with her whistle urging on-lookers to join the merry-go round.

After some time, another dance party came. It was made up of school children and a few adults, who we learnt were members of the governing board. The new party stayed away at some respectable distance, and for a short period, the two groups stood each other in a test of supremacy, each trying very hard to outdo the other. The kids, glaringly disadvantaged in number and quality of performance, suddenly took off in full flight towards the showground. The older group shouted in triumph, and went after them in mock pursuit.

Together with the chief and a few elders of the village, we followed in a walking pace behind. During the walk, consultations were made. I was approached to be the referee, which I tactically declined for obvious reasons. I could not imagine how I would be running around in the swamp, more so as, I had on a pair of leather shoes, purchased in Port Harcourt during the orientation for N35.00, a fifth of my monthly allowance. I was not ready to ruin it for any novelty match. Samuel, who had on a pair of canvass shoes, the NYSC issue, accepted the offer, a decision he regretted later, for his canvass shoes were almost completely ruined. The vice-principal and I were to be on the high table as vice chairman and the guest of honour respectively.

The football field was a perch of land of about one hundred by fifty feet. It was swampy, and because of the heavy rains of the previous few days, was heavily water locked. It was apparent that it was not in regular use: it must have been prepared for the match, as it was still littered with freshly cut grass and shrubs. Some portions were completely buried under water. The school itself was a pitiable shed of three classrooms, if they could be called so. Only one of the three rooms had what could be called walls, and it was obvious the doors and windows had never had shutters.

The Chief made much of our presence during the opening ceremony. He introduced us not as guests from Ukubie, but as guests from, Kaduna, Bendel and Ondo States for Samuel, the vice principal and me respectively. The response from the gathering was electric. Chief Benaebi in his speech also corroborated him. We automatically became the star guests.

The match started after some initial delay. The town could not make up the required eleven, and so wanted the school team to reduce its number to seven. Naturally the pupils protested vehemently. To this argument was added the wish of the school team to have the two members of the village team remove their boots, on the ground that this was unfair advantage. In the end, a compromise was reached: the men were to keep their boots, but should serve only as goal keeper and a defender, and any goal scored by either of them would not count, while the school team should also keep its number.

All along, I had viewed the game as a novelty match. I was mistaken: it was not so with the players and villagers. The heated argument surrounding this initial controversy gave a hint of what kind of match to expect. Each party pursued its cause logically and with all seriousness.

Meanwhile, the spectators, school pupils and town folks, did not stay together around the pitch. The school children congregated on the far side with their drummers, while the town's folks stayed around the high table also with their drummers, an arrangement that was to generate another controversy during the course of the game. As it turned out, we were not the only outsiders on the arena. I could see a handful of our students around the arena. I also learnt that a few people came from some neighbouring villages.

In a little while, the game started. It was a rumble in the mud. Players rolled and wrestled in the swamp. In a question of minutes, every player was covered with mud. I could see why nobody talked about jerseys. You could not tell one from the other. It was only size that told the town folks from the kids.

Samuel, the referee too, had his own share of the *roforofo* splash. He had to remove his shoes after they became mud-logged and too heavy for movement; he also had to roll up his trousers high above the knees.

The town team scored first, but the echoes of their jubilation had hardly subsided before the pupils replied with what was clearly a handball, and which the referee rightly disallowed. The call was met with stiff protest from the pupils. When the high table intervened, the pupils accused members of the high table of partiality, and only agreed to continue play after a protracted argument and rancour. We later learnt that the pupils concurred in deference to us. In spite of such incidents, it was altogether an interesting experience.

The actual match lasted about forty minutes, part of which was spent on protest and wrangling. It came to an abrupt end when the ball, an inflatable type, lost pressure completely. The school had no hand pump, so there was nothing to do to re-inflate it. As soon as the inevitable final whistle went, the two hitherto hostile parties merged in an orgy of celebrations. The two teams, all covered in mud, raced ahead in the direction of the river, followed by children, who cheered them noisily along.

By now, I had started to think of our journey back home. It was already six o'clock in the evening, getting dark. I was not alone; Samuel too and even the vice principal were having apprehensions about how we would make it home. But Benaebi waved our fears away.

"Don't worry," he added exuberantly, "this is an opportunity for you to see another beautiful aspect of Akpoi creek."

"No problem sir," a boy who I later learnt was a student from our school, assured us. He had approached Benaebi for a ride with us back home. His colleagues, we were told, had gone back through a bush path.

In spite of the assurances, I could not still my fears. Travelling at night on these lonely and dangerous creeks was very far from my idea of fun. But what could Samuel and I do? So we all settled down to a lavish feast: food and foreign spirits of various labels assorted drinks were in abundance, and of course the ubiquitous *Apeteshi(*local gin*)* and *Izon wuru(*palm wine*)*. I warned Samuel to abstain from alcohol, because of what I perceived as our rough journey ahead. Benaebi saw through this, and again dispelled our fears. He was in his elements as he went from one joke to the other. The Chief and his people loved it.

At exactly eight o'clock, we announced our readiness to depart, to the great disappointment of our hosts. Some had even thought that since we came from far away states, we would spend the night with them. It was obvious, when we all stood up, that some members of our party were a little tipsy. But Chief Benaebi remained as sober as if he had not taken a drop of wine, which was great comfort to everybody.

We bid our farewells and were on our way. There was no question as to who would operate the boat: Benaebi took full charge, with the vice principal lighting his way with a flashlight. Our fears about the journey home turned out to be largely misplaced, for the return journey turned out to be very refreshing and pleasurable. Even though the way was as dark as anybody could imagine, Benaebi threaded the boat through the dark winding creek smoothly and effortlessly. We almost regretted leaving so soon, for we had left behind a greater part of the merrymaking arranged for us.

We came across some canoes, mostly fishermen and women. We even had time and courage to stop to buy fish from them. There was no secrecy about who we were, and where we were coming from; they all knew we were coming from the football match. Some of them exchanged banters with Benaebi in the local language. We arrived home at about nine o'clock, and settled down in Benaebi's home to continue with the fun. Unknown to Samuel and me, some drinks had been taken to the boat while we were at the chief's place. They kept us busy far into the night.

CHAPTER SEVEN

December was around the corner, and we had to travel out for graduation and Christmas festivities. It was not as if we were eager to travel out. I, for example, would have loved to hang around for the four-week vacation, but for the fact that life in the village would be so boring without the students around. We dreaded weekends and holidays. It was not as if our students did anything in particular for us, but they kept the school compound and even the village lively. The idea of spending four weeks of holiday in Ukubie was like looking forward to going behind bars. So we made up our mind to travel out. About a week or two to our departure, we decided to give ourselves a treat. We went out to buy fish and condiments. I also wanted some smoked fish and dried lobsters to take home. We went through the length and breadth of the village looking for smoked fish without success. We were about giving up when we ran into a girl. She turned out to be Ebitonye, a form four student of our school.

"Good afternoon sirs," she said, beaming with smile.

"Hello," Samuel responded.

It turned out that Samuel knew her. They went into some exchanges during which I moved on but they soon caught up with me. Samuel told me the girl had offered to help in our search for smoked fish. She disappeared, and came back a moment later to inform us that she had located a fish seller. We thereafter followed her, and got all we wanted. She also volunteered to take them home for us. That was the beginning of my relationship with Ebitonye.

A few days later I saw her when I visited Benaebi in his office.

"Hello Ebito…," I said, struggling to complete her name.

"Ebitonye," she completed it for me.

"Thanks for the other time," I said.

"Don't mention sir," she responded shyly, walking away. At that point, Benaebi emerged from his office.

"Is that how to greet your teacher?" he intervened. She stopped in her track.

"What else do you want her to do?" I whispered so that she would not hear.

"A lot more," Benaebi responded in a corresponding low tone.

She came back, and we exchanged some more pleasantries during which Benaebi interjected continually in Ijaw. Even though I did not understand what his contributions were, I felt the effect on the girl's reaction and genuflections. So effective was the later interaction that all the rough edges of coyness and nervousness had been completely trimmed off by the time she finally left.

"You know what we are doing?" Chief Benaebi said as soon as Ebitonye was out of earshot.

"What!" I asked, looking blank, since I could not see any connection between what he just said and the incident that had just taken place.

"You know what! We have just disturbed a wasp nest," he burst into his characteristic infectious laughter.

"Wasp's nest?"

"You have it in your area, don't you?"

"Oh yes! *agbon*," I said, looking lost and stupid. "But what is it?"

"That lady likes you."

"*Hen en*! She is no wasp. How does wasp come in?"

"I can see you don't know her. First, she is a daughter of the village Chief, and second…"

"I thought you were going to say she is the wife of the chief." I cut in, becoming impatient.

"May be that would have been better. You can take anything from this village….

"City!" I corrected him. We laughed and he continued

"City! Yes…but don't touch his daughter," he said. He dropped the piece of information as if he was dropping a red hot iron on my palm.

"I see. Is that all?" I said with a sigh of relief.

"No! There's a more serious one. Even as we are talking now, you can't be too sure somebody is not informing somebody."

"Who is that?

"Somebody's name I am not competent to mention."

"Common! Why don't you come out straight?"

"Your boss has been on that girl ever since he came to this village" he added finally.

"Who is my boss?" I asked. And just as I mentioned the word 'boss', the principal emerged from the school path, coming in our direction. Chief Benaebi smartly put his fore finger on his lips to signal the end of the discussion.

December came, and we left Ukubie. We arranged with the principal to use the school boat to which he agreed. He even consented for the boat to pick us up at Yenagoa on our return journey, but the plan didn't work out because I arrived late—two days of waiting had exhausted his patience, so he left without us. On getting to Yenagoa, our colleagues in Bishop Dimeri Secondary school gave us the message that the boat had left and that we should go by the local transport.

We took *Ayakpor* the following day, and spent two gruelling days getting to Ukubie. The journey took two days because, we were told, the boat developed engine trouble; but we later learnt that it was customary of the skipper to break his journey at Amasoma, to spend a night with his mistress under the pretence that the boat had technical fault. We spent the night with our Youth Corp member friends. We set out around three o'clock in the morning and arrived at about six o'clock in the evening. The journey was not as bad as the previous one, partly because we were used to these unforeseen delays by then.

We arrived at a relatively dry and sunny Ukubie. But for the familiar terrain and structures, I could have sworn it was a different place entirely. The ever present drizzle and marshy terrain were all gone. The school compound too was sprightly and inviting. It was wearing a new look. Somebody had come up with the idea of erecting a fence around the compound, an idea I considered superfluous. A natural fence of dense evergreen forest surrounded the school. There were no animals or humans to keep at bay, as it was conveniently removed from the village. The fence, which was half completed when we arrived, was made of sticks. Bundles of freshly cut sticks littered the grounds. As if to deny us access to our house, there was a large concentration of freshly cut bundles in the frontage. Somebody even had the uncivil audacity of standing a few bundles of the sticks by the wall on the veranda.

The following school day came, and we discovered that all activities had been suspended for work on the fence. Still bubbling with energy and enthusiasm, we joined the exercise and participated actively. We were told the principal had announced that no student should visit any teacher's house. Sometimes during the week, we had asked Napoleon, a friendly Form III student, to buy us a bunch of plantains from the village after school hours. We were having siesta when we were woken up by the loud voice of the principal from his quarters. He was shouting orders to somebody.

"Hey! Boy, where are you going?"

"I want to carry this plantain to the Corpers house sir." It was Napoleon directly behind my bedroom.

"Have I not told you not to visit any teacher?" the principal bellowed.

"They asked me to buy it for them sir," Napoleon pleaded.

"Follow me to my office."

"Sorry sir, I don't know sir, as they are not teachers."

I got up to peep through the window to see the drama going on outside. The principal, looking wild and enraged, was moving towards his office while Napoleon followed behind at a safe distance. Samuel had gone out, and was talking to the principal confirming Napoleon's story. He could have been talking to himself, for the principal did not pay him any attention. Samuel got the bunch from Napoleon, and with a wave of the hand, encouraged him to follow the principal. By then I was out in the sitting-room, taking in the incident with utmost bewilderment. I did not venture to go out; I only whispered to Samuel to come in. Given the rebuttal the principal had given Samuel, I did not see the wisdom in going to plead with him. Since the principal's office was directly in front of our building, we stood in the sitting room watching him and Napoleon.

He came out of the office, and handed Napoleon a piece of paper the content of which sent the poor boy wailing. Napoleon came out of the office and stood on the corridor looking in our direction not knowing what to do. We hissed and beckoned to him to come after the principal had gone out of earshot. He hesitated, and finally moved in our direction.

The note, which was very curt, was a suspension order: "You have been suspended indefinitely for insubordination. You must not be seen on the school premises until further notice." It bore the principal's stamp and signature. We got the note from him and did everything to calm him down. He asked whether he should go home to contact his parents, but we told him not to do so, and promised him we could handle the matter. By the time he left, we had put enough confidence in him to the extent that he could remark that the note could not prevent him from visiting us.

After he had left, we remained in the living room to ponder over the matter. It was clear to us that it was an affront on us. The principal's action was a coded message for us. Even during his altercation with the boy, he had spoken so loudly that, clearly, his words were meant for other ears than Napoleon's. We searched our minds to see if we had done anything wrong, but we could not put our fingers on anything. We resolved to put up a fight. First, we would not raise the matter with him, and if he did we would cold-shoulder him, by telling him that since he was the Alpha and Omega in our Ukubie world, he could please himself.

The event took place on a Friday, so we had the whole weekend to think of a worthwhile line of action, and also inform our friends and some members of staff, particularly, Chief Abraham, who had been a friend and confidant. He promised to raise the matter with him, but we insisted he should not, and if he eventually did, as he insisted, he should not let the principal know that we told him. We also established a strong solidarity contact with Napoleon. He was pleasantly surprised when he saw us in his house in the evening of Friday. We also spent Sunday afternoon in his rented room in the village

Monday came, and it was school time. The school was to continue with the fence work. We decided on a boycott. The suspension order by all logic should be applicable to us. Very early in the morning the centre of activity was right around our house, and that made our absence so conspicuous that students were even asking for our whereabouts. We kept indoors and did not even answer many of our friends, who came knocking when they did not see us.

By one o'clock the vice principal came. We allowed him in, and we exchanged some pleasantries. He told us he had come because he did not see either of us, and thought somebody was ill or something. Apparently the principal had not told him about the incident. Given the good relationship between us, and the fact that he was our next door neighbour, we confided in him, and gave him every detail of what we intended to do.

"This is war," he intoned after a long spell of silence.

"We are ready," I responded.

"We are soldiers," Samuel reinforced my response, nodding his head brusquely in consonance.

"Why don't we do it this way," the vice principal said. "Let me talk to him. Naturally I should be in a position to assure you that the suspension order will be lifted, but … you know when he's like this…."

"Whatever happens, we are prepared. May be God has willed it that it was time we left this bush," Samuel said, his temper rising with every breadth.

We allowed the matter to rest like that and resolved to deal with the issue as it unfolded. Meanwhile, I have not seen Ebitonye since I came back. She asked me offhand to bring something for her from home, and in response to this request, I bought a pair of school sandals, which I was eager to give to her. We stayed off school activities from Monday to Wednesday, but since there were no classes (the school was still busy with the fence), our boycott was hardly noticed.

Our draught gathering became more vibrant and robust than ever. The sessions, which were always at the veranda of our house, were bursting with attendance. Even people, who knew nothing about the game, like Benaebi, were always around to share in the regular jokes. We played far into the nights. A recurrent incident was that the principal would always find course to invite one of the teachers while play was on. None of them ever told us why, and we never bothered to ask.

Benaebi encouraged us in our action, and as we discovered later, we had the support of many teachers. However, the comment of one of them gave a clue to the reason behind the principal's action. I was, no doubt, the best player and I had just finished a winning streak when somebody remarked that he would ask the chief of the village to give me a woman before I left Ukubie. In response another person, a supporter of my last victim, said he would cause the new fence to be further reinforced.

"*Oloruntoba, if you dey play like dis, di chief fit give you a woman before you leave dis village e.*" It was Tebiowei. He knew next to nothing about draught, but his jokes, always biting, kept the gathering alive.

"As a matter of fact, I think I am due for it already," I said standing up to show off. The gathering erupted in laughter.

"Who will give this novice a woman?" my defeated opponent remarked. "If they give him, I will build another fence round this house. There was more laughter, but this time subdued, and accompanied by a sharp exchange of glances.

In the evening of Wednesday, Chief Abraham dropped in to inform us that the suspension order of Napoleon had been withdrawn. He pleaded with us to overlook the incident, and continue with our regular activities in the school. The news came to us as an anticlimax, because we had really prepared for a fight. The vice principal came to us in the middle of the night to brief us about his efforts to resolve the conflict. We thanked him but made him realize that we were not impressed and that we still had an axe to grind with the principal, and would let him know it at the next available opportunity.

Meanwhile Ebitonye proved elusive. Four weeks after I returned from holiday I had not set my eyes on her. I did not make any deliberate effort to look for her. Before we went home for Christmas, we had started preparing for inter house sports. It was to be the first in the history of the school, and since I was the Assistant Games Master, I took active part. This role again brought me in contact with the principal, who was highly excited about the idea, and in no time I was forced to put aside my dislike of him.

The competition turned out to be a huge success. Guests turned up from the whole district, and the village, which had never witnessed anything like it before, was agog. In the evening of the ceremony, after the official refreshment, we went out on a drinking spree. By eight o'clock we wound up action in the village and carried along drinks to continue the festivities in our house.

It was a moonlit night, and you could see well over a hundred feet ahead. Chief Benaebi and a number of friends joined us. Since the completion of the fence, about three security guards had been hired to man the gate with the strict instruction to prevent boarding students from coming out, and prevent day students from entering the compound in unauthorized hours—after school hours.

"Welcome sir!" One of the guards greeted us.

"Good evening," I answered and instinctively handed over the two bottles of beer I carried in a polythene bag. The poor man grabbed the bottles, and headed for our house, which was just a few yards from the gate, thinking that I had asked him take them home for me. Sensing the error, I hollered:

"Where are you going?"

"To your house sir," he answered timidly.

"Don't you take beer? *You no dey drink beer?*" Samuel said.

"*We dey drink sir.*"

"*No be say I give you to drink? Why you dey carry am go my house again,*" I said after a deep belch.

"Drink and enjoy yourself, *na di ting wey we bring from town be dat*" Samuel said, and handed them his half smoked packet of cigarette. They could not believe their ears. They were dripping with gratitude.

We eventually settled down to a long session of merry making. As the night wore on, we ran out of drinks and since it had become a capital crime for students to be found in our quarters, we relied on the security guards to get supplies from the village, an assignment they carried out with delight. However, I noticed that they spoke in low tones any time they were with us, and were in the habit of casting secretive glances in the direction of the principal's quarters. Naturally more tipple and food went to them in appreciation.

By ten o'clock the party had thinned down to three of us, Samuel, Benaebi and me. It was at this point that one of the guards whispered to me that they would like to have a chat with us after all our guests had left. Benaebi took it as a lift-off call, and left.

Two of them came in, the most elderly and the one who ran the errands for the evening.

"*Onua e!*" the elderly greeted in Ijaw.

"*Doo o,*" we replied in unison. We invited them to sit down at this point. I started wondering what the matter could be. I had thought they were just coming in to thank us for the drinks and food, but given the seriousness they attached to their presence, I began to suspect something more serious. In spite of the fact that I was a little tipsy and tired, I brazed up for the worst. My fears were further confirmed when we offered them more drinks and they declined so emphatically that none of us repeated the offer.

"*Sir e, we been wan see you before dis time.*" It was the elderly man again, and the two of them rose up simultaneously.

"Please sit down," I said, stretching both hands to demonstrate the point.

"*We tank you for wetin you don dey do for us dis evening,*" the elderly continued.

"Oh! Is that why you have come? Please don't mention it any further," I said.

"*Na wah o, wetin we give you?*" Samuel added, rising up to signal the end of the meeting.

"*No be di only reason, but sir na only craze dog go get shop wey no go shake tail. You see sir, I tink say na God send you come dis town. Na di day when you come na hin my wife wey never born for ten years born, and na boy.*"

"Is that so?" I interjected.

"*Na true sir,*" the younger man confirmed.

"*Na wah o!*" Samuel added.

"*Anoder one wey pass dat and wey consan all of us,*" he said pointing to his partner "*be say if not becos of you, we for no get dis job.*"

"We! How?"

"*Na so dem dey ask person, sir,*" the elderly man answered. "*My friend go tell the second part of di tory.*" With that he sat down and his partner took over.

"*I tank you sirs,*" the younger man said and insisted on standing. We were then more interested in what he was going to say, so we did not entreat him to sit down.

" *Na true say if not because of you sirs, we for no get dis job. I know say you self for don dey worry say why dem come put fence and guard for dis school. Wetin tief go com steal for di school wey dem no fit steal now self as fence and security de?*" the young man went on. He was the more articulate of the two. He spoke his Pidgin English with native speaker proficiency. By then we had become so fascinated that Samuel thought we needed more drinks. He dashed into his bedroom, and brought out a bottle of Vat 69.

"*As I dey talk sir, di tin wey I dey talk be say no need for fence and security. Na becos of you dem put di fence and na becos of you dem employ us.*

"*Wetin we have wey tief go steal?* I asked.

"*Ha sir, you get plenty,*" he said, exchanging pregnant glances with his partner.

" *Di ting wey you get wey some people here no get be respect and honour. Dey no dey take moni buy am for market. Di ting be say you get am or you no get am. If I tell you someting, you go believe?*"

"Why not? Go ahead! We responded.

"*Di reason dey build dat fence, and put us as gatemen na to prevent women from coming to your house.*" he concluded in a confident lordly knowing manner. He allowed some moment of oratorio silence to elapse before he continued.

"*Na dat be di order wey dem give us when dem hire us. Na him also make dem say make student no visit teacher. You don hear am before: say make student no see teacher?*

"*Na only Ukubie,*" the older guard responded, rising up on his feet to take over in a well choreographed arrangement.

"No! No! No! Sit down," I said with a note of finality he could not resist. "And please pick up your glasses and serve yourselves," I commanded. The two of them had declined taking from the Vat 69 earlier. However, with my order, they changed their minds, and reached for glasses.

"What about your partner at the gate?" Samuel inquired

"No worry sir" He dey wit us. He dey watch make dem no know say we dey here". The older guard responded. *"But di ting be say, since we come here we don dey watch you as you dey do. You no get enemy: everybody na your friend. Even look at us, wetin we get to make us sit down for di same table dey drink wit you. Na him make me and my friends say we no go allow anyting disturb you as you dey here. Any woman wey you want see, student or no student, carry am come, anoder gate dey for your backyard. You go see am tomorrow. Anytime wey you wan see somebody call me or any of my broders, we go call am for you. Egberi fa e."*

This was how we came to learn about the reason behind the construction of the fence and the principal's antagonism towards us. Also the idea of erecting a fence around our house, mentioned by a colleague as a joke during a draught session tied up perfectly. We thanked our new friends and confidants. Up till that very moment, I never seriously thought of Ebitonye as a girlfriend, but the revelations called for a review of my relationship with her. I longed for her. I wanted to see her. I wanted to do anything that would hurt my boss.

I vividly recalled what Benaebi said about my boss and Ebitonye. How did the principal get to know about my brief interaction with Ebitonye? Enemy within! Snakes have hands. Benaebi must have been relating to his friend.

CHAPTER EIGHT

One Saturday afternoon, we were out visiting a colleague whose wife had a stillbirth. Members of staff and a few town folks were there when we arrived, but we could not spend much time there because we could not reconcile the festive mood there with the loss. There was abundance of food and drinks. The only people who showed any semblance of grief were the parents; all others were in such a high spirit that you began to wonder what they would do at a child-naming ceremony. This strange attitude was not new to us; we got the first experience when Chief Benaebi lost the first of his twin babies. We received the news with the greatest shock, and immediately rushed down to his house on a condolence visit, but—incredible!—the family was in such a high spirit that we dared not raise the matter until another person, also there for the same reason, mentioned it. A few months later the twin sister died, and it was again party time. On that occasion I just feigned some illness as an excuse to leave the scene.

This time around, after exchanging pleasantries with the hosts and guests, we withdrew to WACO site to spend some time with Benedict in his porter cabin apartment. We were there for the better part of the day. It was pitch dark when we came out, and going through the village late in the evening, we noticed that there was an unusual heavy human traffic on the village pathway.

I did not pay any attention because I thought it was the eve of the market day, when people from the neighbouring villages came into the village for the market the following day. By the time we got to the jetty side, it was obvious that something more than the market was in the offing. The jetty was crowded with people coming into the village, all of them gaily dressed. They did not look like the regular passengers on the creeks. We could also hear some loud highlife music coming from the direction of the school. I had to reassure myself that I was in Ukubie. We turned to Benaebi's house in want of somebody to talk to, but the place was under lock and key. It soon became apparent that the movement was towards the school compound. We stood by while the stream of humanity continued along the pathway.

Out of the blue came Parabida, a lively, easy-going Biology teacher; he too was in his Sunday best!

"Good evening sirs!" he said in his usual uproarious manner.

"Hello Mr Parabida! How is everything?" we said variously.

"Fine Sirs. Aren't you coming?"

"What's going on?"

"You mean you haven't heard? Something that is happening in your backyard," he said looking genuinely surprised.

"What is it?"

"It's a party sir. I.K. Belemo."

"I.K .Belemo?"

"Yes sir! I.K. Belemo. You should know him sir; he stays in your area-Lagos.

It was the first time I ever heard that name. By now the man hardly needed any further introduction, his music, the highlife type, was all over the place.

"But this is Rex Lawson's music," I remarked.

"Na him pikin." The reply came from a colourfully dressed passer-by.

"Di guy dey popular e. I no know as you no sabi am," Parabida said.

It was obvious at that point that we were a bother to Parabida. He exchanged greetings with his many friends, who passed by, and the exchanges ended with either "I am coming," or "*Na me dey for your* back *so,*" or "*Make I finish wit my Ogas.*" As we were talking, the band was doing an old Rex Lawson popular number, *Ibi na bo.* The music rode above the forest that separated the school and the community, and settled on the village. And apparently aided by nature's echo, it filled the entire surrounding. It was palpable; you could feel it even in your being. It was a welcome change to the noise of crickets and toads that usually besieged you on the ridge-path on a typical Ukubie night.

However, if the experience appeared strange to us, it was not so with the villagers and its stream of visitors. It was as if some supernatural force had come down to liberate some bottled up energy. The old and the young joined in the singing. Almost everybody within our immediate environment was moving towards the music as if in response to some irresistible drawing force. Even an old woman, who, apparently for reasons of old age, would not be making the trip, was humming the tune as she worked on a fishing-net hung out in a line in front of her house.

We got back home to see a new school compound. The entire place was swarming with people. It was as if the entire village had emptied out into the school compound. Right in front of our house were people, men and women, young and old, with belongings flung all over the veranda. They took off as soon as they realised we were the occupants of the place, in spite of our pleas to them to stay. We were in the middle of this when Mr. Tamuno, the vice-principal, in a most colourful traditional dress, breezed in.

"Where have you been?" he asked, radiating a newfound warmth and cordiality.

"What's happening?" Samuel queried.

Apparently, he had looked for us everywhere as soon as he learnt about the impromptu visit of I.K Belemo, but could not locate our whereabouts. According to him, he got wind of the visit of the highlife musician after we had left the house of our bereaved member of staff. The performance was to take place in front of the village Chief's residence, but it was later moved to the school assembly hall when the musician himself got to know about the hall.

I.K. Belemo was on his way to a performance somewhere upstream when his boat developed an engine problem a few nautical miles to Ukubie, and was forced to stop over. Local hands had spent the first day on the repair without any hope of success. While the repair was going on, some folks came up with idea of an impromptu performance, which the band accepted as a welcome relief from boredom and weariness. It was even rumoured that the delay in the repair was contrived by the local mechanics to force him to tarry in Ukubie for the performance. As soon as he consented, words went round the nooks and crannies of the communities in the creeks.

The turnout was overwhelming: it was indeed a gathering of the entire Akpoi clan. The assembly hall was jammed-packed. The turnout cut across the entire social spectrum, from the low to the high. Local chiefs turned out in full regalia, each trying to outdo the other. I counted seven of them. One even came with his royal umbrella, which a hefty man carried open and high above the chief's head, even though it was moonlight, and there was not a drop of rain. It was for lack of space that the umbrella was folded in the hall; otherwise the aid was bent on keeping it open.

We got into the hall around ten o'clock, by which time the party was in full swing. The atmosphere was electric. The reason for Chief Benaebi's absence became instantly obvious: he was in the thick of the organization, soaked in sweat as he dashed from one section of the hall to the other. He was in his elements. As soon as he spotted us, he ushered us into a corner of the hall where he had arranged seats for us. The principal and a few notable members of staff and prominent folks from the community were already there.

The dance party was in three concentric rings; the outer and the innermost rings moved clockwise while the second, the inner one moved anti-clockwise. It was a brilliant choreographic arrangement. The inner ring, which was the favourite of the chiefs and the elderly, was the least active of the three. They took things easy, content with just swaying from side to side. The real action was expectedly in the outer loops, made up of young men and women. The women carried handkerchiefs, which they waved in time with the cadence of the music. It was a copy of the Akpoi experience on a jumbo scale.

The band, hemmed in awkwardly by a motley circle of onlookers, was however a far cry from my expectation, for given the quality of music exuding from the hall, I had expected a grand spectacle, with state-of-the-art instruments. But it was a simple ensemble of five members. The leader, I.K. Belemo himself, was a middle-aged man of average height, dark complexioned with a slightly bulging belly, which robbed the body of any claim to handsomeness. He wore an undersized French suit, which awkwardly amplified his protruding tummy. The remaining four were young men in their late twenties, or early thirties. They all dressed casually—obviously as a result of the impromptu nature of the outing. The instruments were scanty: two guitars, one bass and the other solo, a set of conga drums, and a pair of percussion sticks. They sometimes improvised with oral whistling and click sounds for some special effects.

It was unbelievable that such a ragtag band could produce such an enthralling melody. The strength of the band was actually in the lyrics, which was in Ijaw and since the crowd was familiar with every word, they sang along the refrain, and they could have even drowned the lead singer, but for the amplifier which raised the voices of the band members above the background provided by the participating crowd. The music of Rex Lawson and other notable highlife bands dominated the social life in the sixties and early seventies, even in my own part of the country.

Teachers and students were calling at our table to pay homage. Parabida bumped in his usual swashbuckling manner, and demanded why we were not on the dancing floor. It was a joke directed to Samuel and me mostly, and the import was not lost on the rest, for soon after he left, entreaties were directed at us. And before we knew it, the vice-principal was on his feet and with arms stretched, invited us to the floor. An over enthusiastic observer slotted each of us into gaps in the outer ring, and we joined the merry-go-round. As if to welcome us to the floor, the band switched to the popular *Ibi na bo* number. It brought back memories of my old secondary school days. Our presence in the dance circles drew unusual attention. Students and town folks alike exchanged banters with us.

"*Oga you dey dance?*" a fish seller in the village remarked, waving her handkerchief at me.

"*Dance emi e,*" I retorted in Ijaw, alluding to her usual response to '*Ndi emi!*', meaning, 'Fish is available'. The immediate dancers around us burst into laughter. I was just recovering from the effect of that joke when Parabida sauntered across from nowhere. He stood directly by my side, and cupped his mouth with his hands as if he was going to divulge some secret to me:

"*Hi be like say I go go home go bring my wife.*"

"*Go quick,*" I replied instinctively.

He withdrew, still looking at me from a distance, and laughing his head off. The reality of his joke about bringing his wife soon dawned on me when, a short while after, I looked back to talk to Samuel, and discovered that the lady directly behind me was Ebitonye. It was more than I bargained for. As I learnt later, the whole idea of dancing was planned, and put together by Benaebi. Moments after, when he came around to inform us that the drinks he sent for had arrived, I could see the monkey business engrained on the smile on his face. And from that moment, all I wanted to do was get out of the ring, the dancing floor, and even the hall. It was a big relief when the band wound up for a recess. As soon as the music stopped, we made our way out of the floor to join

Benaebi and the rest. The principal, we were told, had taken leave of the table. He probably must have found the whole arrangement embarrassing for him.

The table had taken on new members. Teneni, Ajaji (pronounced Azazi), Isaac 'Black Dog', the school accounts clerk and a few town folks had joined. Standing sentry behind the group was Stephen, the senior security man. He was all smiles, his face betraying the encounter we had with him and his partner on the night of inter house sports competition. I greeted him and he answered with an awkward martial salute, which drew a loud laughter from the onlookers.

We settled down to enjoy the drinks we had ordered. Belemo, the bandleader, soon joined us. Introductions were made, and from the very moment Belemo learnt I was from the Western part of the country, he took to me, and we were soon engaged in discussion. He wanted to know how I was coping in the community. He viewed my situation with pity. Every effort to let him know that I was doing well, and that there was not much difference between the environment and where I came from, left him unconvinced. He viewed my situation with pity, and came up with suggestions about how I could make the best of the circumstances. When I happened to look up, I discovered we were the focus of attention of the entire gathering. All the while his fans and admirers, old and young, formed a ring around us. Stephen kept himself busy by keeping them at bay. For his efforts, Benaebi handed him a bottle of Guinness stout, from which he drank conceitedly while using his crude baton to restrain the crowd from getting too close.

"*No where wey you stand wey you no go see dem,*" he counselled the children, who formed the inner edge of the circle of on-lookers.

Belemo gestured to him lightly to take things easy .We talked on a number of topics ranging from music to politics, particularly the total neglect of the Delta community He told me about his late boss, Cardinal Jim Rex Lawson, his efforts to keep his legacy alive, and his love for Lagos. His simple appearance belied his resourcefulness and wealth of experience. I shared with him my love for his brand of highlife music, which the late Rex Lawson epitomised. He gave me the background story of my favourite number, *Jolly Papa*. I also revealed to him my earlier ignorance about the language of the lyrics.

Like most people in the western part of the country, I had thought the lyrics of Rex Lawson's music was Igbo, whereas it was Kalabari. It did not surprise him when I confessed my ignorance to him: he was quite familiar with it. He added that people outside the Eastern Region even regarded them, Ijaws, as Igbo. We discussed the glorious age of highlife music and the exponents like Fela Ransome Kuti, Victor Olaiya, Roy Chicago and a host of others. I was amazed at his knowledge of the social life of Lagos and the Yoruba ethnic group. He believed strongly that highlife music would come back. Even though the brand of music was no longer fashionable across the nation, it was still very popular among his people, the Ijaws, who even regarded it as their traditional music. The reception that night was an expressive testimony. I did not share his optimism, however.

A member of his group came to give him some information. The import of the message soon became clear as he suddenly came alive, and announced that his boat had been fixed and could be leaving any moment from then. This was bad news for the gathering and the new development spread like wild fire among the crowd, who at that point were superlatively primed for more partying.

As usual, Benaebi was at the head of the delegation put together to persuade him to extend the show. Seeing my new relationship with him, Benaebi tactically got me to put in a word, which I did. At last Belemo obliged to stage another short round. By now the gathering was exceedingly lively. Jokes and repartees flew freely. Our adventure on the dancing floor and the accompany drama took the front burner.

I was planning to avoid the heat by leaving the hall under the guise of going outside to take fresh air when the band struck the chord for *Jolly Papa,* my favourite number. Without being told, I knew it was a special number for me, and to confirm my suspicion, Belemo looked in my direction with a come-on smile. It was all the invitation I needed to go to the dancing floor. By my judgment, it was the virtuoso of the entire performance. The horns added some irresistible out-of-the-world sonority. The lyrics flowed, as I had never appreciated it before. It was Cardinal Jim Rex Lawson resurrected, and an everlasting seal to the short encounter I had with him. I was almost transfixed as the music reverberated and locked in my subconscious. I felt as if there were only the two of us in the hall. He punctuated the original lyrics, which was Ijaw, with panegyric chants in English directed at me:

"*This number is dedicated to our honourable Youth Corper*s , *…who have come from far away land to serve our father land… So shall a man leave the comfort of his native soil… to live among people of different culture to serve his country… Thanks for coming to live among us. We appreciate the sacrifice. We love you. God bless you… etc, etc.*"

With the mention of Youth Corps, the crowd was no longer in doubt as to who the number was intended. Fellow dancers on the floor, particularly the elderly men and women, shook hands with us. It was enlivening,

Rumblings of thunderclaps and a sudden influx of people from outside the hall signalled the arrival of rain. Lightning flashes riveted into the hall through the open windows. The music became somewhat suppressed, with the rain and lightening providing a strange but matching background. It was the sign-off call for Belemo. The music quickly lapsed into jazz and conga frenzy, as if in competition with the intruding forces of nature. Belemo disappeared from the stand. The weak and the elderly vacated the floor, leaving mostly the young folks, who were bent on savouring the last bit of the fun. The music went exceedingly lively, and the dancers responded with matching brawny steps while the rest of the crowd, now lined along the walls, egged on the show with clapping and catcalls. The orgy went on until about three o'clock in the morning when, exhausted, the band finally wound up to a tumultuous end.

CHAPTER NINE

It was another Friday, meaning another dreary weekend ahead. This one would be very dull indeed, as three of our key draughts players would be travelling out of the village. Teneni, my second in command, as we called him, would be travelling to Port Harcourt to attend to urgent family matters. 'Black Dog' would be going home for his grandfather's final funeral ceremonies. We had planned to accompany him all along, but the carefully arranged logistics went into a hitch when the school boat we had banked on broke down on the return lap of the principal's monthly trip to Port Harcourt. Nicholas, a not-too-good but consistent and upcoming player, would be visiting his wife in a fishing port somewhere along the seashore.

It was with the sad thought at the back of our minds that we went to the school assembly that afternoon. It was to be a short one as there had not been any major event or issue during the week. Amadala, the teacher on duty, went through the rituals of prayers and announcements hastily in tune with the demand of the occasion, and was about to dismiss the gathering, when the principal walked in to announce that the end of term examination would commence the following Monday.

The students went into spontaneous shouts of "No! No! No!" while teachers exchanged glances of disbelief. He further announced the names of teachers who have been assigned special responsibilities, like timetabling and question paper production, vetting and coordination. My unusual calmness must have prompted Samuel to ask whether I knew anything about the development.

I replied calmly, "Me! No!"

The two one-syllable words had hardly left my mouth when Mr. Amaso, a brash and loquacious Mathematics teacher, asked to know when the staff took the decision to start the terminal examination the following Monday.

"Why don't you allow me to finish so that you can have plenty of time to make your own announcement," the principal said without even looking in his direction.

Silence reigned.

If Samuel believed what I told him about my lack of foreknowledge of the development a moment ago, the next announcement from the throne raised a doubt.

"Mr. Oloruntoba will oversee and coordinate the mock examination of final year students," the principal said, looking in my direction for confirmation. Anybody listening to him could easily have concluded I was privy to the decision. I maintained my silence and cool.

The assembly dismissed on a rancorous note. The students continued to register their protest in loud chattering, while members of staff maintained pregnant silence. The principal left just as he had come in, not talking to anybody, even those he had assigned responsibilities, leaving behind an atmosphere of intense intimidation. After some respectable distance to the hall, the teachers broke into groups of twos and threes, obviously trying to make sense of the development. I was very sure within me that none of them was privy to the principal's arrangement. Even Chief Abraham, the oldest teacher, believed to be the principal's right-hand man, wore a blank and vacant look while the announcement lasted. If he had had any foreknowledge of it, he would have been fretting and whispering, as he was wont to do in such situations. Instead, he looked impassively stupid.

Samuel and I walked quietly to our office, which was the third room to the principal's in a block of rooms. On our way, we passed the staff common room where some of our colleagues were discussing animatedly, most of it in Ijaw. A few loaded remarks were thrown at us through the window, but none of us replied in any meaningful manner. In the office, I sat on my table swinging my legs in consonance with the thoughts rioting in my mind. Samuel was going through a recurrent round of recriminations punctuated by fits of grunts and hisses. He was going mildly berserk and it was all I could do to calm him down.

I took mental stock of how far I had gone with my final year class where I taught English Language and Literature-in-English, and also of the ground still to be covered in Form Four, where I also handle the same subjects. In none of the two classes had I reached the point where I could honestly call the students to write the terminal examination.

It was not that I had not performed my duties properly. It was just that all along there had been all sorts of impediments strung along the course of the term, which prevented full-time serious work. To start with, it was still well over a full month to the end of the term and, furthermore, we had spent most of the time on frivolities. For instance, we practically went on holiday any day the market fell on a school-day, and any day Ayakpor, a store boat, arrived was generally taken as a free day for the students, a fact I learnt in a very funnily bizarre manner. I was in the middle of a Literature class one afternoon when I suddenly noticed some kind of restiveness among my students. It all started when I heard some distant hooting—apparently of a boat. In less than fifteen minutes my class had emptied out by half! And yet I did not know when the students left, either singly or in groups! So how did it happen? Unknown to me, each time I turned to write on the chalkboard, one or two students would leave the class, as quietly as possible, through the nearest convenient exit - window or door.

Things came to a climax when the student who asked a question, that necessitated my writing on the board, disappeared before I turned round again. I went livid with rage. I decreed a moratorium on any further movement and ordered the class captain to produce his missing mates within minutes. When I ventured out of the classroom to let off steam by walking on the veranda, I noticed, to my amazement, that the entire school compound was virtually empty. A class one student loitering around the building told me Ayakpor had arrived, and that the entire student population and staff had gone a-shopping at the jetty. When I realised my mistake, I lifted my moratorium, and apologised to the remaining students for my ignorance. The apology was not needed, for before I finished making it, the rest had all flown past me, racing to the jetty to meet Ayakpor.

I finally resolved to challenge the principal on the sudden rescheduling of the terminal examination. I got down from the table and sat down to scribble a memo lodging my formal protest. Meanwhile, Samuel continued his grumbling and petulance. I finished the memo and passed it on to him to go through. He brightened up, and went for his pen to append his signature. I made him realize that he should allow me to make it a personal affair, since the issue I addressed had to do with my direct interaction with my students; and besides, I would not want a situation where the principal would be going round saying that the Youth Corps members were challenging his authority. I wanted him one on one. He agreed with me, and I took the note to the principal's office and handed it over to him. He fleetingly went through it and jauntily said, "That is all right." The memo was mild in tone. All I said was to the effect that since I had not covered the syllabus and rounded off my lessons with my students, it would be professionally improper for me to ask them to sit for examination as requested by the principal. The memo said nothing about lack of consultation, which was the main reason for my discontent.

Some teachers called at our office on their way home, and they registered their disenchantment with varying degrees of vehemence. Some vowed not to prepare questions, while others, particularly the elderly ones, saw the issue as being in line with the principal's style of administration, which they were used to. Amaso, the one who asked a question in the hall, was a raging ball of fire. Not only would he not take part in the exercise, he would physically assault any teacher who participated in it.

"I will come with my letter of resignation on Monday," he raged.

"Why would you lose your job because some self-conceited individual lacks basic management etiquette?" Samuel asked coolly.

"No! That is if the worse comes to the worst."

"Nobody will lose his job. It's going to be a decent boycott." I added evenly.

"Whatever you people decide to do, I will join you, but make sure that once you start it everybody must be steadfast. . . no backsliding, no compromise. Because at my age. . . ," Chief Abraham said and left. He had stayed around to listen to opinions of other teachers.

What was started in our office spread like a wildfire. By Sunday afternoon it had become the talk of the village. Benaebi accomplished the bulk of the spread. He chewed and chorused the words *boycott* and *sabotage,* having picked them up from our discussions, as a child repeats over and over a new word.

An event was to happen late that afternoon which not only further strained our relationship with the principal, but also gave him a piece of what we were capable of doing. We got home that afternoon, had our lunch and withdrew to our different bedrooms for our regular siesta. I was reading the last chapter of James Hadley Chase's *One Bright Summer Morning* when I heard knocking on the front door. When I opened the door, it was the principal's nephew, Kehinde.

"*Principal say make I call you. He be like say you get visitor. Na bot of you e,*' she said, beaming her characteristic smile and zoomed off. I called Samuel out and gave him the message. We were about to leave when a teacher dropped by to give the same message, this time adding the identity of the 'visitor': some NYSC official was in the principal's office to see us. With the edge to his words, he must have thought he was doing us a favour by alerting us so that we could prepare to meet them in good shape. As it turned out, he was to be one of the backsliders in our approaching encounter with the principal. He was actually in the principal's office to pledge his loyalty indirectly—by asking for examination materials.

"*Na wah for dis people e. Dey tel you say dey go come?*" he said in low tone, betraying some urgency and fear by the way he was fretting and genuflecting. He stood up periodically to look in the direction of the principal's office. He must have got the shock of his life when we decided not to honour the invitation.

"If they are from the NYSC Secretariat and they want to see us, they will come here," Samuel said.

"You are very correct. So we don't need to go hustling there," I completed the thought for him. "Thank you Mr Tebiowei"

"*Make I go tell dem?*"

"Please yourself," I answered him, and with that we got up and went back to our respective bedrooms to continue our siesta. Mr Tebiowei could not believe his ears.

"*No do so e. dis people de very wicked e,*" he pleaded, almost reaching out for Samuel, who by then was at his bedroom door.

"Don't worry Mr Tebiowei, we can handle them," I said, practically putting an end to the conversation as he was becoming bothersome.

No sooner had he left than there was another knock on the door. It was expected, so I went out again to answer it. Just as I emerged from my bedroom into the sitting room, the principal barged in offensively.

"Did you get my message?"

"O yes."

Almost immediately, one Mr Addey of the NYSC Secretariat in Port Harcourt emerged behind him. He was no stranger to me;

I knew almost everybody in the secretariat. I had had course to deal with him when I was trying to change my posting. He was a generally loud and pompous individual.

"Hey you! Don't you know I am from Port Harcourt?"

I was still searching for a correspondingly rude answer when Samuel interjected from behind me.

"So what?"

"Who is this? Do you know who you are talking to?" It was vintage Addey.

"So because you are from Port Harcourt we should be keeping vigil to receive you," Samuel said turning to go back to his room. I stopped him by pulling his arm.

"Mr Addey, I don't think you are here to see us. If you came from Port Harcourt to check after our welfare, your first port of call should have been here. Look at you. I pointed at him. You even feel too big to enter this place. My colleague here is from Kaduna State and I am from Ondo State. You can compare the distance to your Port Harcourt"

Addey was not made to receive such battering. He was vibrating with anger. His eyeballs were sweltering balls of fire—a pitiable spectacle. He let loose some wild grating noise, and vanished from behind the principal just as he had come. Left with no other option and apparently embarrassed, the principal also left.

The Addey incident came and went in a flash. Nobody made any reference to it thereafter until our time was up, and it was time to report at the NYSC secretariat in Port Harcourt.

CHAPTER TEN

The build-up to the strike took on a dimension I never envisaged. For us, it was a simple way of pointing out an administrative incontinence, but for the staff and even students, it was a rare opportunity to take on a leadership that had treated them with scorn and disdain. It was an opportunity for them to formally challenge and force the autocrat of a principal to recognise them as credible partners in the smooth-running of Government Secondary School Ukubie. As it turned out, it also threw up some individual personal agenda, some of which were to shape the course of the entire struggle.

Chief Benaebi launched himself into the fray as if he was a member of staff. He indeed had every right to act so, for he taught in the lower classes on a volunteer basis. To most students, there was no difference between him and regular members of staff. He apprehended and punished students, and even because of his relatively higher social and economic status, commanded more respect among students than most teachers.

Monday came and went just like any other school day. There was no examination, and the principal did not make any attempt to enforce his orders. However, one or two teachers prepared questions and attempted to submit them to him. We learnt that the principal asked them to hold on to their questions. Final year students made an informal representation to me, as the coordinator of the mock examination, to ask for a shift. I told them I had no such powers, and directed them to the principal.

The position of the vice-principal in the whole affair was indeed complicated and pitiable. From his actions and utterances, we knew that the principal did not consult him before his announcement, even though he claimed he told him shortly before the assembly. He nonetheless remained loyal to his boss. He did his best to persuade us to drop our protest, but we refused, and did everything to avoid his company. We even had to cancel our regular draughts session for the weekend, because he was always present as a spectator—in any case, most of the players were out of town.

Tuesday and Wednesday also went like Monday without any major development, but normal teaching went on. Towards the end of Wednesday I had an attack of malaria, and so left the school before closing time. By virtue of the close interaction among members generated by the boycott, the news that I was ill spread faster than normal. By the evening many members had called to see me. Naturally, it was an opportunity for us to share views about the action and to reaffirm our individual commitment to the cause, since I was emerging as the rallying point. By the evening, I had succumbed to the recommendation for a massage therapy, which had been the parrot-cry of almost every visitor I received, and it was the responsibility of Benaebi to produce an expert from the village. I specifically requested for his father, who was the best in the community, but the old man himself was under the weather, so he went for a substitute.

Massaging was the village's cure-all remedy. Malaria, headache, diarrhoea, and many other minor ailments! Massage cured them all! It was very effective, they claimed; but I never believed them, and had never thought I would one day be subjected to it, but what to do now?

They had other health care methods, which were also suggested but which I declined. Everybody was his or her own doctor. Every family had its own reusable hypodermal syringe, and there was a rich supply of drugs, both oral and intravenous. One afternoon, as we were taking a walk across the village, we came across a small crowd in front of a house. In the middle of the crowd, a girl lied prostrate held by two hefty men. A third man had in his hand a syringe with which he was withdrawing fluid from a coconut. He subsequently gave the poor girl several shots of the coconut fluid. Upon inquiry, we were told the girl had an overdose of some drug, and she needed the treatment to calm her down. Even when there was no means of injecting an intravenous drug, it was applied orally. According to a local folk, "*Na the same body hi de go.*"

The therapy turned out to be a painfully refreshing exercise. The masseur, who was a very funny individual, doused much of the pain with his jokes. He was never short of them. He went from one to the other. He would tap one part of my body and screech, "*hey na soup dey here so!*" or "*Beke ynash!(Whiteman's bosom).*"

The exercise went on for about an hour and into the night, during which those who came to commiserate with me joined us in the room. We remained in the room well after the masseur had left. Benaebi had left mid-way through the exercise, and never came back. Black Dog, who went home for his grandfather's burial ceremony, seized the opportunity to entertain us. Drinks and snacks were brought in, and before we knew it, we were having a party.

By 10:00 o'clock, the last of our visitors had left and I was just settling down for a blissful night sleep when Samuel came into my bedroom to inform me that Ebitonye was in the sitting room to see me. I was at sleep's threshold when he came, so I was not sure I heard him properly. It was the stuff fairy tales are made of. I did not believe him.

"Which Ebitonye?" Did you say Ebitonye?"

"*Which one you dey now*, the same Ebitonye," Samuel replied, looking confused.

I got off the bed and struggled into a pair of trousers and T- shirt. This was a strange happening by all consideration, and completely out of tune with all known logic. Chief Benaebi and I had done everything—pulled every trick to entice her, but she had proved unresponsive and elusive. I had in fact given up on her, but somehow the residual flicker of love kept burning in my breast. She took my breath away each time I saw her; and her disobliging attitude had not diminished my longing for her. Once when we were in Benaebi's office, he sent her half-sister to tell her that he had an urgent message for her. She came, but the moment she realised I was there, she turned her back and sprinted out of sight in seconds. But there she was, now, in my sitting-room, and all of her own volition.

I came into the sitting room treading carefully; still wondering what manner of trick Benaebi must have pulled to get her into that house. She perched on one of the chairs, and became a little uncomfortable when she saw me.

"Hello…,"I managed to say, holding back the remaining-*"What Angel brought you here?"*

"Good evening sir," she answered, looking away from me.

"Nice to see you," I said. It would not only be unreasonable but criminal to ask her what brought her, which was what occurred to me to do next.

"I hear say you dey sick."

"Oh thank you. Is that why you came?"

"I hear from one student, as we dey go home in the afternoon, but as dey say make student no enter your house na him make I no come den."

If I had any happy moments in Ukubie, that hour was the greatest of them. It became even more pleasing to know that she came of her free-will.

"How did you get here?"

"Haa! I walk now. Taxi no dey for Ukubie"

"Did you see the security men at the gate?"

"They are there."

"And they did not ask you any question?"

"Dey ask where I dey go. I tell dem say na vice-principal send for me."

"I hope no one else saw you." I asked these series of questions to make sure the principal did not see her, as it would mean providing him with a weapon to roast us. To be caught with a female student, the village's chief daughter, at that period of the night, would do our cause no good. I was still thinking of a worthwhile topic to raise when she spoke.

"Sir o, di main reason wey make I come na di ting wey dey happen for school. Since Friday, different people don dey come see my fada and na all of dem dey mention your name. If dis one talk finish he go say na Oloruntoba, if dat one talk finish na Oloruntoba. No be say dem talk say you do any ting bad o, but dem dey talk am say na you and principal. Even your friend businessman don dey come too." Her soothing velveteen voice floated tenderly in the air, scaled the gulf between us, and went down deep into the recess of my heart.

"I hope dey no say we want to kill di principal." Samuel interrupted.

"No, but as dem dey mention your name, di principal no fit like you and he fit do someting bad to you," she said with a note of anxiety to her voice.

"Well Benaebi should be able to explain things properly," I added with a note of assurance.

"I tink say you know say your friend is a businessman," she said, with the ring of anxiety turning to cynicism. By the time she finished, she was on her feet. We rose in response.

"Thank you. God bless you," I said and promised her we would be careful and reassured her that we were not doing anything to hurt anybody. Sensing that she was about to leave, I dashed into my bedroom to bring out a flashlight. She declined the offer, and even prevented us from seeing her off beyond the door. As soon as she was out of sight, I dashed to my room, where I had a clear view of the security post. As if in readiness for her arrival, the three security sentries gatemen were standing right at the entrance in what looked like a guard of honour, and as she approached they eased themselves out of her way. If verbal exchange went between them, it could only have been an exchange of greetings, for she neither stopped in her stride nor looked in their direction. I went back to the sitting room to inform Samuel of my observation. We were rest assured, at least for the moment, that the principal would not know about the visit. With that assurance we went into our separate bedrooms for the night. At about 7:00 am the following morning, Samuel woke me up. I was taken aback by the look of anxiety on his face.

"What is it?" I asked as I struggled out of bed. I became more anxious as he waved me back in to my room. Naturally I thought it was a development from Ebitonye's visit the previous night. But it had nothing to do with it. According to Samuel, the principal had been shuttling between his house and the vice-principal's house, and he had overheard some comments, which made some surreptitious reference to us. Such comments were: "I will show you that I am an Ijaw man," "No stranger can do me any harm," "On my father's land?" etc. Samuel thought that such comments, uttered at the precincts of our house, were directed at us and for our hearing.

His fears were far from being misplaced as the events, which unfolded rapidly, that morning proved. Just as we were settling down to decide on what line of action to take, the vice-principal came in. He did not wait to be received in the lounge, but came directly into my bedroom. He barely knocked at the bedroom door, and as he entered the room, without mentioning it, his mission became obvious. He offered the normal pleasantries, his eyes roaming the corners and crannies of the room, hardly making any eye contact with any of us.

"How is your malaria?" He reminded me of my sickness, but which the massage therapy had cured, and therefore hardly remembered even by me.

"Oh! Well I am fine."

"I want to see somebody in the town. I just thought I should see you before I go," he said, as he craned his neck to see beyond a side cabinet.

He went out just as he came in. We became more confused. Was he in some sinister league with the principal?

"Have you seen Benaebi...?" Samuel asked in desperation. "Sorry I was just...," he retracted the question when he realised it was very early in the morning, and there was no way I could have seen Chief Benaebi.

We decided to wait for whatever was coming. Inwardly, I felt like seeing Benaebi. He had left in the middle of my massage treatment the previous night, and had not bothered to know the outcome, which was very unusual of him. We came out of the house to the veranda to discover that the whole compound was empty. This was most unexpected. Students should be coming in by now. Nevertheless, I drew Samuel's attention to it, who expressed the same mild anxiety. We decided to wait and allow things to unfold and react accordingly. Just as we were settling down, Boniface, a loquacious Form III student came in, and as usual, started his repartee.

"*Oga na here you dey? Town don scatter e.*"

"What!" "*wetin?*"

"*The fire wey you start don dey burn. Amo! You mean say you no know anyting?*"

Samuel and I stared at each other. As soon as Boniface saw the seriousness on our faces, he calmed down and gave us a brief account of how '*town don scatter*'. The story was that we, Samuel and I, were planning an attack on the principal, and that we had spent the previous night amassing weapons, and mobilising members of staff and some students. My bedroom, the story also had it, was the war office and armoury combined. We burst into laughter simultaneously. It sounded so ridiculous that we were wont to pass it as one of the boy's rude jokes. But inwardly, the connection between what he said and the vice-principal's early morning visit was not lost on us.

"*I tink you don knack your ogogoro dis morning*," Samuel said reaching out to give him a slap. Samuel withdrew only when he did not attempt to dodge the blow as he would ordinarily have done. He took the feeble slap on his back without a whimper.

"*Oga na true e. The whole village dey in front of the village chief house now- now as I dey talk.*"

That was all we needed to get the gravity of the situation into our body chemistry. We were enveloped in fear, but also fired by anger. It was as much as I could do to keep my hand from shaking. Samuel's large eyeballs were like flaming balls. They would start dripping blood any moment. They bored into my half frozen forehead for possible explanation that was not there. I saw a flicker of doubt in his bearing.

"I- know – nothing – about - this," I said, looking at him directly and shaking my head slowly in agreement with my dragging voice, and opening my palms in cadence with the utterance. He believed me. Of course, he had no other option, because apart from the fact that I was ill, and remained indoors throughout the previous day, we were together almost all the time. There was no way I could have been involved in such a plan and kept it away from him. He sprang unto his feet, and started prancing the length and breadth of the sitting room as if ready to pounce on an invisible enemy. That was his method of letting off steam. I was used to it by then and knew how to handle it. I pretended I did not see him, while I engaged Boniface with some searching questions about the happenings in the village. He fed me with details, like who and who were out there and the general reaction of the villagers. Everybody was surprised that a simple school affair could degenerate into such a serious confrontation, but according to him, the general mood was against the school authority. After some time, Samuel calmed down and joined us. We shook off the initial shock and braced ourselves for whatever was to come.

Just at that moment the vice-principal passed through the frontage of our house. We could see him through the two large windows of the sitting room. He did not even look in our direction, let alone exchange greetings with us. He hollered to his children, and said something in Ijaw, which Boniface interpreted to mean asking them to stay inside the house because the compound was no longer safe. He again appeared at the window and went past without paying us any attention.

At that stage we decided also to leave the school compound because we felt it was no longer safe for us, too. But there was the problem of where to go. For all we knew at that point, the whole village was against us. First, we sent Boniface back on a reconnaissance mission to the village, specifically to look for Benaebi and explain our situation to him. As soon as he left, I suggested that we should each scribble down some note; something the outside world would see in case anything happened to us. Samuel entitled his own 'to whom it may concern', while I addressed my own to Chief Benaebi. I packed a few things in a handbag: like spare clothes, shaving kit, some tins of milk and my bible. Samuel saw the wisdom and did the same thing. He brought out a bottle of whisky from his room and we settled in the sitting room waiting for the worst.

After what looked like eternity, Boniface appeared along with two Form V students, Napoleon and Fineface. Together they gave us an accurate and up-to-date account of the crisis and what was happening in the village. Apart from some minor details and fill-ins, which they supplied, it was largely as Boniface had reported earlier on. The principal, in a save-our-soul fashion, had approached the village Chief for protection against an impending attack orchestrated by members of the National Youth Service Corps and his regular members of staff. He had earlier in the day declared a school-free day to enable the chief carry out his investigation. The announcement was made through a town crier, which explained the non-appearance of students on the compound that morning. The chief consequently summoned his council of chiefs to deliberate on the matter. Some members of staff had been invited to testify, and none had owned up to having knowledge of such an intrigue so far. A few had even sworn on our behalf that nothing of the sort happened, and had insisted that the principal should name his stool pigeon. Benaebi was nowhere to be found. Nobody had sighted him that morning, not even members of his household could tell of his whereabouts.

Rather than allay our worries, the confirmation of Boniface's earlier story further increased our fears. We quickly, though in a friendly manner, dismissed our student friends, not because we did not appreciate their effort or their company, but because seeing them in our house and in our company might be misconstrued as evidence that we were indeed mobilising students to carry out our purported plan. And of course they might be marked down for victimization by the school authority.

A little while after their departure, we set out for Benedict's place, which was at the extreme end of the village. We avoided the normal route, which would have taken us through the village. Instead, we went through a bush path behind the village. I once took the route with Benaebi when we were searching for his half-brother houseboy, who ran away from home to avoid punishment. It took us directly to our old house, a stone-throw from Benedict's portal cabin. He was in fact about to leave for our place when we arrived. We did not need to do much briefing for he already knew everything. We only gave him our own side of the story, much of which he new anyway. He asked whether any of the regular teachers had been to us that morning, and when we told him we had not seen anybody apart from the vice-principal and the three students who came to our house, he became a little agitated and decided to go out on a fact-finding trip to the village centre, which we never thought necessary, but not before we had had something to eat. We had almost finished a whole bottle of whisky, which Samuel bought earlier in the morning, on an empty stomach, so in spite of the fear and anxiety, we felt the need for food.

After a meal of boiled yam and *peppersoup*, Benedict set out on his reconnaissance mission. We settled down to review the strike action and the events of the day, and mapped out our next line of action. Left alone, Samuel was through with the village. If Ukubie had not been a communication-locked village, hardly could he have waited for Benedict before taking off. I did the best I could to persuade him against such an action. The irony of the fact that it was I who had been bent on leaving upon my arrival in the village, who was now persuading him to stay, was not lost on him. He did as much as blame me for coming back, for if I had not come back, he probably would have found his way out of the hell too.

"*You fit wait make dem make you the chief of the village, for me na go be dis,*" he concluded with a note of finality.

"Let's see what is going to happen".

"*I don hear.*"

"You never can tell."

"*For dis jungle! Wey somebody dey manage to stay.*"

Persuading him not to go was a pure academic exercise, as there was no means of carrying out his threat. Unless one ran into the likes of Sea Truck, which were few and far between, the only commercial boat was *Ayakpo*, which only passed through Ukubie once in two weeks. Even then one would be lucky to get a space as it was usually full to the brim before reaching Ukubie.

Benedict came back with a load of news. It was as if our friends and foes alike were waiting for us to leave home before calling at our place. He saw everybody except Benaebi. Both the principal and the vice principal were out looking for us. He saw five members of the draughts group loitering at our veranda as if in preparation for a session. He called at Benaebi's place, but his step-brother-cum-houseboy said he travelled our very early to Gbaraun on a business trip, which sounded strange to me because he did not tell me anything about it. Acting on his own initiative, Benedict did not tell them about our whereabouts. According to him, the general angst and anxiety of the early morning had simmered down considerably, or so it seemed, for the crowd in front of the chief's house had disappeared, and villagers and students were no longer in groups discussing the crisis.

However, there was little we could make out of the finding, as the information did not touch the heart of the problem. For instance, we still did not know how the principal learnt we were going to attack him and what has been done to allay his fears, and if the fears were still there what would be his next move. Collectively, we decided to stay put in Benedict place, and let whoever wanted us do some searching.

Benedict did his best to make us comfortable and secure. He made sure nobody came in. He met and dismissed all his visitors at the door. Chief Abraham came about noon, not necessarily to ask for us, but to intimate Benedict with his misgivings about the stories making the rounds in the village about the scheme to attack the principal. He never expressed any regret about being part of the boycott action, but was particularly peeved about being listed as one of the persons plotting to attack the principal.

"How can I, an old man like myself, plan to go and attack Penane. My fourth younger brother is older than him. If you saw the way he was making mouth today. Anyway I need to see Oloruntoba to know exactly what happened."

"I am sure nothing like that happened," Benedict chipped in.

"Ojigo, the man who massaged him yesterday said all the time he was in his room nobody mentioned anything like that."

"So Ojigo went there to massage Oloruntoba?" Benedict asked.

"Yes now. I was there myself throughout, throughout! Nobody even talked about the boycott," a third voice contributed. It was Teneni, a member of the draughts group. He was passing by and overheard the discussion and decided to join them.

"I didn't even see Ojigo. I only went in briefly to greet him when I heard he was sick," Chief Abraham said.

"Why did he refuse to mention the person who told him before the chief?"

"Was his friend there?" Chief Abraham asked.

"He was there. Where else would he be? Samuel was there all the time."

"Not Samuel. I mean Chief Benaebi, Businessman."

"No be him bring Ojigo? But he no stay for long."

"Alright, we will know the truth," Chief Abraham said and left.

"I am sure it's all a big lie," Benedict said as the other parties left.

As soon as they departed, Benedict came in. He did not need to do any reporting as we heard everything. In fact it was only the thin aluminium wall of the porter cabin that separated Chief Abraham and me. It was with much restraint that we did not come out of the cabin to join the discussion. The chips were gradually falling in place. Two possibilities offered themselves for consideration: it was either the principal himself or somebody else who saw the massing of teachers in our house and interpreted it to mean we were plotting an attack, or some mischievous person, who was in my room, deliberately lied to the school authority about the purpose of the gathering.

"What do we do now?" It was Samuel with a ring of edginess to his voice.

"I think you should stay here for some time. In another hour or so I will go out again to see if there's any further development. At the end of the day you will discover there is nothing to the whole story," Benedict counselled.

"I think we are just giving these people unnecessary credit. Left to me, we should just go there and let them do their worst. *Haba!*"

"My worry is not so much about what the principal will do, but about the teachers. If they found out we have gone into hiding, they might begin to think that our hands are not clean after all."

"Ha- haa! You see!" Samuel quipped.

"All the same, let them look for you for some time. They may also think you are hiding because you don't want to be attacked."

"What do you think, Sam?"

"OK now. *I beg you no get drinks for house?*"

With that, we settled down to another round of drinking. Benedict began to have a string of visitors. A few of them were students and members of our staff, who came mostly to inquire about us. They all claimed to have been to our place, but found the place under lock and key. Others were town folks, who came for business totally unrelated to us. One of the former group, a member of the draughts group, wanted to know if Benedict had seen us that day, and gave a hint of the rumour making rounds in the village that we had left the village. He said some women claimed they saw us leaving through the back wood path. Benedict made a good job of warding them off at the door. He always ended by saying he was on his way to our house to find out for himself.

CHAPTER ELEVEN

By eight o'clock in the evening, we decided to go home, but we agreed never to divulge our hiding place, since doing so could put Benedict in unnecessary discomfort. We put together a neat story about trekking to Akpoi, through a bush path. It would not going to be difficult for anybody to believe, since the rumour was already going round that we had left the village in fear, and some women had actually claimed they saw us on our way to Akpoi.

We arrived the school compound into the waiting hands of the entire staff of Government Secondary School, Ukubie, a large number of students and a handful of town folks. The news or rumour about our disappearance had engulfed Ukubie like a rampaging thunderstorm. What we conceived as a little hide-and-seek game turned out to be the masterstroke that resolved the entire crisis and further refined our relationship with the school authority, and Penane in particular. The principal, who like a saint had approached the Chief's assistance in resolving the crisis, was then seen as a villain, who had, through his high-handedness, driven the godsend Youth Corps experts away. In no time, the chief, his council and the local people had seen through the principal's allegation, and ruled his entire story as a lie. The staff and students must have done a thorough PR job educating the villagers, for they knew everything about the crisis, even as much as any member of the school community. The principal himself wondered why he fell for such a false alarm.

However, he still held on to the source of his information: he would not disclose the person who told him we were planning to attack him. The teachers, with the assistance of some students, had searched every nook and cranny of Ukubie, even as far as Lobia, a market village some distance away, but without any clue to our whereabouts. Even if they had continued till kingdom come, there was no way they could have found out our hiding place because our host, Benedict, was not only in touch with them, but also offered them suggestions that kept them away from his porter cabin.

As soon as the crowd spotted us, there was a commotion. Shouts of "we have found them", *tank God e we don see dem*", "Oga Oloruntoba" etc, rang out all over the place. People expressed happiness in various forms, and the shouts reverberated throughout the village. We were thoroughly embarrassed. Even though Benedict had briefed us about the anxiety generated by our disappearance, we never expected people to show so much concern. Even people we had never had any form of relationship with leapt for joy when they saw us. Almost the entire school population, student and staff, was on hand. I suddenly found myself fighting back tears. Samuel was doing the same thing, and in a more visible way.

Following the lead supplied by the women who saw us in the morning and reinforced by Benedict's suggestion, a search party was about taking off to Akpoi when we showed up. We entered our house together with as many as the sitting room would hold, mostly teachers and students. Nobody pressed us for any explanation, but we thanked them for their concern and asked, in passing, if we were safe at least till the following morning, to which everybody reacted spontaneously. "*I beg e, you no dey go anywhere.*" "The devil has been put to shame." "*Na di devil go go, no be you e.*" The reactions were instructive in a strange way. As far as we were concerned, the principal was the devil, and he was there giving approval to these calls if only through body language. I started wondering who this devil was.

By 10:30, the last of our visitors, Benedict and Napoleon, left. The vice-principal had wanted to hang around longer, but Samuel showed his disapproval somehow rudely, and he left. We reviewed the events of the day and withdrew into our bedroom for the land of Nod for a well-deserved rest. One puzzle that kept nagging my mind was the disappearance of Benaebi in the whole affair. I hoped that by the following day everything would become clear.

About thirty minutes after total silence had descended over the school compound, between wake and dream situation, I heard some persistent faint tapping on my window. Flying termites, which were common in the area, usually made such noise, but it must be early in the evening and the room must be well lit. In no time, it dawned on me that somebody must be behind the window. All the fears Samuel expressed about our safety moments before descended on me, and I involuntarily hollered to Samuel. I got down from my bed on all fours crawling towards the door. Apparently Samuel did not hear me for there was no sound from the direction of his room. It was when I was reaching for the door handle that I heard a faint feminine voice, and I intuitively knew whose voice it was: Ebitonye. I got up from my prostrate position and moved towards the window. I raised the curtain to see Ebitonye, her figure against the thick black night, her eyes a pair of ruby sparkles against the dark night curtain. I dashed across the room to the door and into the sitting room to open the front door for her. I must have made some noise to wake up Samuel for he was there right behind me when Ebitonye stepped in. She entered the room with the same coolness she had tapped on the door moments earlier. Samuel must have been surprised just as I was and was the first to talk:

"*Na you!*"

"*Yes, you dey fear?*" The fear on our faces was obviously as plain as broad daylight.

"Not at all. Come in," I mumbled in relief and surprise.

"*Na wah o.* This is very kind of you." Samuel came to my aid.

"Where is he?" I said looking towards the door, expecting Chief Benaebi to come in her wake.

"Who?"

"The Chief" I have always relied on Benaebi to see her, and naturally I thought he must be behind the night call, but I was wrong.

"*Na me alone.*"

As we talked we gravitated towards my room. And as we did, I remembered the last so-called meeting there which got us into the present travail. The repetition was also not lost on Samuel, too, who jovially remarked that we were withdrawing into the situation office. Looking at her, it did not appear as if it was the same girl I had hunted for months without success. She appeared to have taken on a few more years, and her carriage and disposition, even visage, reflected more maturity and bearing.

"Where have you been?" she asked as she nestled on the only chair in the room.

"We went to Akpoi," I said. This was not the time to tell anybody the truth.

"*Na Akpoi we went o. When your principal wan kill us,*" Samuel said in a matter-of-fact manner.

"Which Akpoi? *You no go any Akpoi.* I asked my sister to keep watch over you all the time. *She no tell you say I go come?*" She must be right because even in the hubbub that accompanied our arrival, I did not fail to recognise a soft voice that whispered something like that into my hearing, but which the general noisy atmosphere must have drowned.

"*You tink say na joke.*" It was Samuel again still trying to sell the Akpoi story.

"*Hi good as you make dem dey look for you. The principal done nearly die. Na so he dey parade my fader's house.*"

"Is that so? What was your father's reaction? Did anybody believe him?" I asked.

"He tell am say make he go look for you. He don tell am before say na him cause the problem."

"Wait! Have you seen The Chief today?"

"Your friend Businessman? *Nobody see am e.*"

"He must have travelled. . . I think somebody said something like that." Samuel chipped in, and with that he rose and left the room. He had earlier indicated his intention to move to the kitchen to boil some rice for us.

" *Why he no go travel, no be business he dey do?* "Ebitonye said sarcastically.

"I am sure if he was around all this would not have happened. You know we have not heard from him ever since he left this place yesterday. He never told me about travelling."

"Why he no go travel? You no know say di man wise pass you. I no talk education. I know say you don go university come. I no know self wheder di man go school. You know say he's not from dis town, Na so so cunny cunny he dey take live him life for Ukubie. He been wan build house for dis village for a long time way dem no allow am. He be like say you no wan hear any bad ting about him. But make I tell you, wheder you like or not, na him make I come for dis night: Na him tell principal say you wan kill am."

"Haahaa! That is a dangerous thing to say."

"Dangerous! *You no know anyting. All dis people way come here tell you say dey no know? Na him tell am.*"

This was an angle I never thought of. Why would Chief Benaebi do such a thing? It sounded so astonishing that I did not even feel the urge of going to the kitchen to inform Samuel. Nobody ever mentioned anything near it, but how did the principal and the vice-principal get to know about the gathering in my room? Why would the latter suddenly turn against us? What was behind his suspicious early morning visit? Above all, why has Chief Egypt Benaebi remained incommunicado ever since? These were troubling questions, among many others, that tugged at my mind, and which only Ebitonye's bombshell could answer.

"Are you sure?"

I dashed into the sitting room to share the latest with Samuel. It was too much for me. He was there on a chair in deep slumber. I thought it would be unfair to disturb him: he needed the sleep more than the bombshell. He apparently used the rice excuse to leave my room to allow me have a free time with Ebitonye. Just as I was piloting him to his room Ebitonye appeared behind me indicating her intention to leave, which I never expected.

"You mean you are going?"

"*For this night*! It's too late now," Samuel said as he walked unsteadily towards his bedroom. I bid him goodnight and returned to Ebitonye standing in the middle of the sitting room. After much persuasion she accepted to stay the night.

The principal called very early in the morning, accompanied by his first wife, and full of apologies in his usual bland and formal style. Samuel at first refused to come out of his room, but after much persuasion from me, he came out—though it was a very scornful Samuel that came out. He just sat there looking like the wrath of God. It was only the entreaties of the principal's wife, and perhaps also my genuflections and body language, that softened him a little bit. He just sat there, giving occasional grunts and rude remarks when the principal touched on some point that irritated him. The principal's presentation did not help matters. He just gave us a chain of actions and reactions of the previous day, such as the information that we were planning an attack on him and his S.O.S to the village Chief. He would not mention the person who gave him the wrong information, not even when I told him we would be compelled to believe he made up the allegation if he refused to name the source. Events however took a more precariously and lively turn when Chief Abraham showed up. He had missed our home-coming the previous night, and had come to say hello, but seeing the principal there, he thought he should bare his mind about the entire affair. The principal went off the handle, and gave him the bitterest part of his tongue. It was much as we could do to prevent them from coming to blows. Even the principal's wife, who had maintained a calm and motherly posture during our discussion with her husband, now rose in stern defence of her husband, and would have physically assaulted Chief Abraham if Samuel had not been alert to restrain her. We finally succeeded in getting Chief Abraham out of the scene. He went away threatening that the principal and whoever his informant was would have to give him a public apology. The shouting match and accompanying uproar invited a few passersby, including the vice principal, our next-door neighbour. We had to temporarily—permanently, it turned out—shed our aggressive posture to douse the tension. The principal and his wife left, but the vice-principal waited a little longer to give us his own version of the imbroglio, and apology as it were.

It was a school day and students and staff were already streaming into the school compound. A staff meeting was called for ten o'clock that morning. For reasons that were not explained, the principal did not attend. The vice principal did a nice job in dousing tension, appealing to us all to forget the happenings of the previous week, and allow peace to reign. Strangely, none of the teachers too spoke in direct reference to what happened the previous day, or did as much to confront the authority. They all towed the line 'thrown' by the vice principal by glossing over the real issues. Everybody appealed to us, Samuel and me, concerning the issue of the previous day. To round off the meeting the vice principal announced that the examinations would commence on Monday week, and went over a new arrangement, which was essentially a rehash of the principal's earlier schedule with minor adjustments. I was appointed the coordinating officer. My protestations were drowned in a sea of appeals from other teachers, including those who had played active roles in the boycott. We wisely interpreted that to mean the end of the strike action.

It was not difficult to confirm that it was Benaebi who was responsible for the crisis of the previous day, as Ebitonye had claimed; but nobody was ready to say so, at least publicly, and his conspicuous absence from the scene came to me as a cruel confirmation. Henceforth, Benaebi avoided us—me in particular—as night avoids day. Some other grapevine stories of my relationship with Ebitonye, real and fabricated, were making rounds in the community, and they all bore the imprints of the businessman.

However, Chief Abraham would not allow sleeping dogs lie; he made good his threat to seek a public apology, and he went about it in a grand traditional style. One bright afternoon, we were reclining in our sitting room after lunch, when Ebitonye sent her sister to inform us that a spectacle we would not like to miss was going on in the village square, which was the village's chief frontage. We hurriedly went down thinking it was a traditional religious or cultural event—I even went with my camera. True, there was a large crowd, and in the centre stage was Chief Abraham addressing the crowd. Since he spoke in Ijaw, we had no idea what he was talking about. If we had been observant enough, however, we would have noticed that the crowd gave our arrival some special attention. Upon arrival we noticed general murmuring in form of interpersonal restive exchanges, but we interpreted that as a reaction to what the speaker was saying. We never realised we were part of the dramatis persona, and important members for that matter. Some students had joined us the moment we appeared from the distance. The accounts clerk, Mr Azazi, came to us and not only intimated that we should be sitting somewhere in the centre of the circus, but was actually going to lead us to the place. Alas! It was Chief Abraham getting his pound of flesh, a public apology. It was our location in the crowd that did not give us a full view of the characters in the inner circle of the crowd. The principal, the vice principal, the consulate officer, the village chief and his chief-in-council were seated—all the bigwigs of Ukubie were seated! Chief Benaebi, a pitiable psychological wreck, was there on a stool set aside from the rest in the centre of the circle, a scapegoat. Chief Abraham was blustering and flexing his muscle as far as his small stature would allow. It was his show, and he was running it well. He demonstrated some added excitement and body movement as soon as he spotted us.

On sighting us, the village secretary—so they called him—came to ask us to take our rightful place in the inner circle. He was not pleased with our refusal, so he went to a higher authority, the village chief. We did not wait for the 'court summons', however, for we took off as soon as we saw what he was about.

We learnt later that Chief Benaebi was made to stand in front of the crowd to own up to his misdeeds and apologise in the traditional form, and pay the traditional fine. It was the most humiliating and debasing experience anybody can go through, with the kids jeering, scoffing and booing. According to the account, he tried at first to give the impression that Chief Abraham, the complainant, was not involved in the scheme, thereby giving the impression that there was a plot indeed; but the gathering saw through it and compelled him to own up that the entire story was a fabrication. Two members of staff came out to declare our innocence and that of other members of staff. Ojigo the masseur was compelled to state his own side of the story. He revealed how Benaebi had earlier told him about a plan by some teachers to cause havoc in the school by beating up the principal, and wanted him to monitor events and discussions in my room, but that he never heard anything about such scheme throughout his stay in my room.

The examination went smoothly without any incident. The staff gave their fullest cooperation. Supervision and grading of scripts were done with dispatch and utmost efficiency—something hither to unknown in the school. The bond and camaraderie that the boycott generated among us was carried into the examination supervision, to the extent that that the principal had to remark openly that it was the best examinations he had witnessed since he got to Ukubie three years earlier.

CHAPTER TWELVE

It was the beginning of a new term, and the end of second term holidays, which meant a new lease of life for us. The previous three weeks had been the most harrowing period of our sojourn in Ukubie. We had decided to stay around during the holidays because of the shortness of the break. It was no use travelling home and staying for just two weeks, and this, coupled with the trauma of a trip from Ukubie to Yenagoa, did not make even a visit to Port Harcourt inviting. We knew what it meant, but we decided to face the odds.

It was as if everybody and the elements connived against us. Almost everybody we had any social acquaintance with left the village for one reason or the other. The draught group was terribly depleted to the point that I almost forgot the draughtboard existed. Ebitonye, who at the point had entered into a full relationship with me, chose the holiday period to visit her relations in Cameroon, and our next door neighbour, the vice principal travelled home with his entire family. The principal, who had earlier on promised us a trip to the Atlantic, left even days before the holidays to attend to some urgent matters in far away Lagos. As if rubbing in our consignment to the solitude and idleness that awaited us, they both asked us to look after the school compound. What was there to look after in a desolate compound? To compound the situation, it was the peak of the raining season. Apart from a few hours which, added together would not be up to one day, it rained throughout. For over a week or so, the sun did not show up at all; it was so dark that you could not tell morning from afternoon or evening. It was a long, bleak holiday indeed!

Soon our apartment, which hitherto had looked like an abandoned property, was again bubbling with life. As students and staff trickled in, we regained our buoyancy. It was as if the holiday had lasted a full year. As soon as the principal arrived, we reminded him of the trip to the Atlantic. He received the idea with much enthusiasm, and it was the consensus that we should embark on it before full activities started. We agreed on a day, the second Saturday of the term. We could have made it the first Saturday but the school supply of petrol for the term had not arrived, and it was not possible to source fuel locally. We did not need any counselling to know how to prepare for such a journey: our rips from Yenagoa to Ukubie had adequately prepared us for the trip. The principal however advised us to come out in light dresses, and take along some snacks for lunch. What he forgot to mention was our life jackets, which we had dusted and kept ready the day we agreed on the date. The vice principal and Benaebi were also billed for the trip. However, for obvious reasons, Chief Benaebi failed to show up when the time came. In spite of the ugly incident that had happened during the boycott and the subsequent strained relationship between Chief Benaebi and us; we all missed him. His absence was a yawning vacuum as long as the trip lasted. But if the principal had deliberately set out to look for a worthy replacement, he could not have gotten a better person than Mr Eseimokumo, who he had asked to join us simply on the account of his familiarity with Koloama—he was an indigene of the area. He too was a very lively individual, and knew the place—the geography, the people and the culture—like the back of his hand.

The school boat was a small boat fitted with an outboard engine. It was a double-decked piece which had, on the lower deck, a bed, a refrigerator, a cooker and a small bed. The refrigerator and cooker were out of order, and as the principal said, nobody has ever tried to use them. The boat was an exclusive preserve of the principal; no teacher ever asked for its use. The story was told about a teacher who once attempted to borrow it to transport his colleagues to the naming ceremony of his child at some neighbouring village. He got more than he bargained for: "the boat is not meant for every Dick and Harry," the principal thundered, and hired him a canoe. From then on, the teacher got his nickname Mr. Dick or Mr. Harry, depending on whether you were a teacher or a student: if you were a teacher you were likely to call him Mr Dick to tease him, but students generally called him Mr Harry, most of them not knowing the origin of the name.

The principal, the vice principal and Mr. Eseimokumo were already waiting for us by the time we got to the jetty. As expected, our life jackets were the first point of discussion as we arrived. Everybody else thought it was superfluous to take them along, but we thought differently. We were both dressed in our NYSC uniform with the face caps. We got into the boat with the one local chap behind the steering, and set out. There was not much of a difference between the boat and what we already knew. We proceeded at a the very high speed of about ten nautical miles an hour in open stretches and crawled where the creeks became dangerously narrow.

Soon we arrived at Lobia, a market village, but since it was not a market day it looked forlorn and empty. But unlike Ukubie, it was not surrounded by heavy evergreen forest; the surrounding was open and bright. A jetty, market stalls and a few huts were all that were in sight. It was not my first time in Lobia; I had visited the place in company of Chief Benaebi on one of his business trips. Minutes after Lobia, it was very easy to recognise the change in vegetation. There was just one dominant type of vegetation: mangrove, more mangrove; mangrove everywhere. I loved it and asked the operator to move the boat to the bank to enable me touch the plant.

"Oh! You mean you have never seen this before!" It was Eseimokumo in a very jovial manner, and just as Chief Benaebi would have put it. "That is mangrove tree, our rich source of firewood.

"I have only read about it."

"It's very good for firewood," the principal educated me.

"And railway slippers," I added, drawing on my Geography lessons of old. The creek became wider, the water cleaner and bluish. As if in magical response to Eseimokumo's mention of the word firewood, two canoes loaded with freshly cut mangrove wood appeared in the distance. They were paddled by some three old women. The canoes were so loaded that they barely remained afloat. They exchanged some pleasantries with Eseimokumo and the operator, who apparently was familiar with them. Eseimokumo brought out a water bottle from which he drank. When Samuel asked him why he could not drink from the river directly, he and the operator responded simultaneously that we were in brackish water, which is not suitable for drinking. To confirm the claim, I bent over the edge of the boat to have a taste of the water: it was pure salt.

The scenery was a far cry from the crowded and damp atmosphere of Ukubie area. Travelling on the upper part of the creek beyond Lobia market is like going through a dark tunnel, with impenetrable thickets of undergrowth and tall evergreen trees, which in most cases practically screened off the sun. But here it was bright and comely. The overriding light green colour of the mangrove blended with the sky-blue colour of the water to complement the tranquillity of the atmosphere.

"Why would people prefer to settle at Ukubie area rather than this place?"

"That is a very serious question," the principal said.

"You mean you like this area better Ukubie?" Eseimokumo asked.

"Of course," I said.

"I think people just settle where they find themselves," Samuel remarked.

"*Oga if you settle for dis place wetin you go dey chop?*" The Operator asked.

"You mean no human beings live here?"

"People live here, but as you will see, there are not many people here as you will find in the upper area. The land does not support agriculture because of the salt content of the water, and it is not easy to get drinking water. The only other plant you will get here is coconut, around the fishing ports," the principal explained.

"*Fish boku, but man no go chop fish alone,*" the Operator added.

"I see."

"But the most important factor is that the land belongs to some people. So Ukubie cannot just come here to settle." The principal concluded his lecture

"You forgot to add that the land is also very rich in oil," Eseimokumo added.

"The bulk of the oil from this state is from this area." The principal added.

"*Oga you touf e, you say make Ukubie people just dey come here*" It was Kekemeke, the operator, who has suddenly developed an unusual interest in the discussion. "*Na cutlass we go take settle am.*"

"He is from Koloama," the principal quietly volunteered

"*No be so government dey come take our oil go dey build Lagos!*"

"Government owns everywhere now," Samuel said.

"*Na government get everyting? Alright we go know when time reash. Make somebody sit down for Lagos dey come tell me say na hin own my backyard.*"

"Why is he so particular about Lagos?" I asked quietly.

"*No be di place di headkota of Yoruba people? Na dem wise pass everybody.*"

108

At this point, the discussion was getting too lively. The principal winked at me, and I understood that to mean a call for a halt to the discussion.

It was fortunate that I read the principal well, for it was the moment the operator decided to give vent to his anger.

"I dey here dey suffer, one person come dey carry my property go sell dey get money. Time never reash. When time reash nobody go tell di beke man wey dem send to go." Kekemeke was now angry beyond placation, and his irritation went into his handling of the boat. *"If not because of di yeye people wey dey represent us here. After dey don chop, dey no dey remember anybody. All of dem! All of dem!. We go deal wit dem.* He banged on the steering wheel repeatedly as if the boat was in league with his imaginary adversaries.

"Softly," Eseimokumo intoned.

"I sorry sir. Di ting dey really pain me".

He stopped, but for me, the atmosphere of intimidation he had created was overwhelming. It was as much as I could do not to express it openly. My fears were now twofold: first, the river had become so wide that I was getting nervous; second, if the operator should suddenly discover that I was Yoruba, the principal and his vice might not be able to prevent him from throwing me overboard! And even then, though the principal and the rest, apart from Samuel, were not in open agreement with him, it was very obvious they had sympathy with his point of view. After he had stopped his vituperations, he relapsed into portentous silence. He would not make any contribution to subsequent discussions or even move in his seat, he just steered into the wide expanse of water before us, while his rage and frustration sent the boat revving in its full capacity. However, the saving grace so far was that he had not realised I was Yoruba. I knew this because on one occasion while he was making his barbed comments he had focused his gaze on me inquisitively as if I was a partner in his distress.

Samuel, sensing my fears, winked at me, got up and headed inside the boat expecting me to follow. I ignored him because

I thought it might be dangerous to leave the enraged operator with the rest of the party—even though they had not openly supported him, they could take the advantage of my absence to inform Kekemeke my identity. If any misfortune was going to happen, I wanted to face it headlong. And besides, I thought my presence was an *in terorem* safety device. Samuel must have read me correctly when he discovered I did not follow him, for he came out a short while after. I there and then decided not leave the three of them together out of sight as long as the trip lasted.

A change of topic and attention however came when Samuel spotted some strange jellylike substances in the water as the boat cruised along, and it was a big relief when Kekemeke volunteered to explain. They looked like cellophane sacks of different sizes and shapes. They were not completely new to me. I had read about jellyfish and similar creatures, but I had never seen them before. The operator described them with great relish, and in a lordly, knowing manner. It was important that he spent much time on it to purge his mind of the pent up anger, so I kept throwing questions at him—some of them actually stupid. For instance I wanted to know if we could catch some to take home, which evoked laughter.

"*Jelly fish na bottles of water. Fisherman wey take jelly fish go home no know say na water he go chop sleep?*"

"They are like single celled organisms, if you break them into bits all the bits would develop into individual jellyfish," the principal contributed.

More relief came when we arrived at what was described as a fishing port, a group of four or five huts on stilts by the side of the river. The huts were actually on the river, for even though there was no water then, the stilts suggested that at some point the place could come under water. There were some tall coconut trees against the ever-present mangrove vegetation, which suggested the permanence or at least non-temporary nature of the settlement. Five women and some children in front of the huts constituted the population as at the time of our arrival. The women sat around some fire, over which there were fish strung together with sticks for smoking, while the children played happily with broken fishing lines and empty cans. The remaining population, we learnt, were out fishing in the open sea.

Moments after our arrival, it would have been very difficult for an observer to believe the boat pilot had been one of us: so completely had he blended into the environment, flora and fauna. He engaged the women in an endless discussion, and even at some point disappeared behind the huts, but even then his voice could be heard as he hollered comments and questions at the women. We soon learnt that his eldest wife was one of the women out fishing. The reason for his excitement soon became clear; he was actually on the trip to take some supplies to the wife, and to collect some of her catch for sale at home.

As we resumed our trip, he took over the task of explaining the fishing port culture. This started when I asked why there were no men in the fishing port, and if there were, why did they leave the women alone at the port.

"*Which man go come sidon for fishing port, na woman fit do dat. Na only Ilaja man fit do dat.*"

"Why now?" Samuel asked.

"Your job as a man is to buy your wife a canoe, and give her some money," Eseimokumo volunteered.

"*After you don do dat, you don do your duty. After dat na to sidon for home dey enjoy.*" Kekemeke added.

"The women stay here for about three months fishing and smoking their catch. They sell to buyers, who come here from the neighbouring communities like Bendel and even Ondo states." The principal, sensing the incoherence in his explanation, went further: "The woman then takes the proceeds to her husband at home and comes back after a short break."

"When does the woman take care of herself?" Samuel asked.

"*No be buy hin husband buy am?*" Kekemeke proclaimed. *As na him husband get am, anyting wey hi get na di husband get am.*

As di husband dey collect money he go dey take care of everybody. He go build house, he go buy clot. All di work wey dey house na him dey do am. Heh eeh, every ting don finish now. Di money wey I go take from my wife today, na zink I go take am buy. When I finish di house, na who go dey live inside?"

"Why can't the husband come down here and do the fishing?" Samuel followed up.

"*Na Ilaja people dey do dat. Man dey fish, but not dis kind; na go-come type.*"

I was not about to forget my worries about the strong views expressed by Kekemeke regarding his perceived exploitation by the Yoruba people. I did not lower my guard for a moment. Even while the discussion about the fishing port culture went on, I knew I had to ensure that the discussion did not veer to an area that could rekindle his enragement.

We saw other fishing ports along the way. They were all as wretched as the first one, and since we already bought enough fish from the first one, there was no need to call at any other one. It was not yet time for lunch, but the sight and smell of smoked fresh fish called for an early one. The fish was '*di-head-no-dey-reash-market*', and Kekemeke readily supplied the reason for this quaint name. According to him, the flesh is so delectable that any fisherman who catches it, no matter how pressed for money he may be, will want to have a taste of it. Most fishermen reserve the head for themselves, sending the body to the market for sale, hence the name. In addition to the fish, *apopo gaari* , unripe pepper and salt, all of which were also procured from the fishing port, were carefully laid out on the deck, and before long we were all at the table.

Even though I was familiar with each of the items, except the variety of *gari*, which was not the type common in my area, the combination was utterly incongruous to me, and also to Samuel. We therefore at first limited our partaking to the smoked fish alone. The fish lived up to its billing. It turned out to be so appetizing that we concluded it would go with anything. We therefore needed no further persuasion before we started reaching out to the other items.

"*Na so dis ting dey sweet?*" Samuel remarked after a few mouthfuls.

"*Oga na our jollof rice be dat e,*" Kekemeke answered.

By 1:30 pm Koloama appeared on the horizon; the rumbling of the ocean waves also became the background to our discussions, meaning that we needed to be louder than normal. There were actually two Koloamas: Koloama 1 and Koloama 2, both separated by about a mile of lagoon water. We never went beyond Koloama 1, which we were told is the larger of the two, but we could see the other one faintly in the remote distance. As we would learn from our guide and host, several years back, there was only one Koloama, but it was the action of the ocean waves which broke the old Koloama into two—as the wave action intensified each Koloama drifted away. Our guide claimed the distance was a swimming distance when the old men of the present day Koloama were young, and that some of them actually swam across to Koloama 2 when they were young boys. He even noted with a sense of regret that they have started noticing elements of divergence in their language.

Our guide and anchorman was an old friend of the principal, an indigene of Koloama, a vivacious, lanky man probably in his late forties or early fifties. Even though he had no notice of our coming, he welcomed us as if he had been expecting us for a long time. He had a habit of folding his nimble frame into a chair with his two legs tucked in beneath him any time he was not on his feet. A few minutes in his zinc-walled house showed that he was not happy with the poor state of Koloama, and like Kekemeke, he linked the deprived condition to government neglect, even though he was not as rabid in his protestation as Kekemeke. Our effort to conceal our identity did not pay off as our NYSC gear readily gave us away.

"*As I dey look you so, I say na who be dis wey dey come arrest me wit police man e?*" he said, looking intensely at me.

"Oh! oh! These are Mr Audu and Oloruntoba. They are members of NYSC in our school."

"I see. *Una well don my broders,*" he said as he effortlessly uncoiled from his chair to shake hands with us in turn. "*Welcome to Koloama e. I tink una don see where government put us. Na so so suffer we dey e. Government no dey come here unless to arrest.*"

"I just thought they should not leave Ukubie without getting to Koloama," the principal added.

"*Tank you my broder. You do well.*"

"Mr Oloruntoba is from Ondo while Audu is from Kaduna," the vice principal added.

"*Amoo! Tank you . Una welcome. God bless you as you come see our place.*"

"*We no dey arrest people,*" I said.

"*My broder, na joke I dey joke. Na your side I dey. Wetin I do wey dem go arrest me? Snake no dey go prison,*" he said as he gracefully folded back into his wicker chair.

His house was constructed of zinc like Chief Benaebi's apartment, except that it was constructed as a full-fledged house, with rooms, ceiling and veranda, etc, and not as a storehouse. The house was built on a raised platform even though there was no likelihood of flooding, to keep the zinc wall from the corrosive action of salt; but even then, signs of rust were beginning to show at the lower end of the walls. He would soon embark on total remodelling of the house as evident in the bags of cement stacked neatly in one corner of the sitting room.

Koloama was not located directly on the seashore, but by a lagoon that sort of sheltered it from the action of the rumbling waves. The tide was at its lowest ebb, so we were afforded a large and expansive view of the beach. Kekemeke, who had disappeared as soon as we arrived, was there at home with some village folks, who were giving him a lesson on the versatility of a newly built fishing boat. The folks shifted their attention to us as soon as we arrived. Poweigha was very proud of us, and he introduced us to his folks as they approached to know our identity. The principal and *Eseimokumo* were the authority of Government Secondary School Ukubie, while we were government representatives from Lagos.

If any of the folks had any grudge against the Federal Government in far away Lagos, they never showed it. They were generally friendly, and the kids warmed up to us. Two of them in particular stayed with us, and wanted us to take them to Lagos.

"*Oga I go follow you go Lagos e.*"

"*Me too I go follow you.*"

"That's alright. What class are you?"

"*I dey primary four*," the first boy answered.

"Why don't you finish schooling before you go." Samuel counselled him.

"*Me I no dey go school, I fit go now.*" It was the second boy, who by then was feeling neglected.

"*You no dey go school!*"

"*I never start*," he responded feeling confused.

"*Na crayfish hi dey follow hin mama cash*," the first said with air of superiority.

"What is your name?"

"My name is Funkeye," the first boy again said, even though the question was directed at the second boy. "*When I reash Lagos, I go change am to Funke.*"

"But *Funke na woman's name for Lagos.*"

"*Woman! Hi no mata.*"

"*My own na Fineface. I no go change am.*"

"*All right I go come take the two of you when you finish school. But Fineface you must start school right now.*"

" *Dem no dey go school for Lagos?*"

"*If you no go school, you no go fit live for Lagos.*"

"*Heh I go start school when I reash now.*"

"You must start right away."

"*I go tell him mama when hi come from fishing port*," Funkeye said tamely.

As we were chatting with the boys, my attention was caught by what looked like some dark shade creeping over the leeward end of the beach. Accompanying the phenomenon was some hissing sound coming from the same direction. The kids burst into some laughter when they noticed my anxiety, and sprinted in the direction.

Our host, who also noticed our consternation, explained that they were crabs coming out to feed. By the time we were half-way to the location, the boys had brought two specimens of the 'dwarf' crabs' to show us. They were a species I had never seen before. They were about a quarter of the type I was familiar with and there were thousands of them. What was interesting about them was that they behaved and acted in unison. A shout brought all of them to a total stop and a hush. Their movement was also synchronised. They stopped as we moved near them, each of them raising its pincer claw, which was longer than the other, only to resume their movement as soon as we were some respectable distance away. And as we moved out of their way they covered almost the entire area not covered by humans and started feeding on insects and worms on the shore.

We tarried a little on the beach to savour the beauty of Koloama shoreline. In the far away distance were dark specks, which we were told were fishing boats, apparently from the various fishing ports. Many of them we learnt stayed about two to four days out in the sea before bringing their produce in. Later we retired to the house of Poweigha, where we were lavishly entertained. We couldn't enjoy his hospitality as much as we would have loved to, having filled our stomachs earlier on with *apopo gaari* and '*di head no dey reash market*'. You could see his love and enthusiasm in everything he offered us.

"*Oga you dey enjoy here o*," I said after taking a highly tasty spoonful of *peppersoup.*

"*We tank God my broder.*"

"Everything is fresh. It will cost a fortune to get this in Port Harcourt."

"You mean this fish?" he asked.

"Everything—the environment, the peace, of course the fish and crabs."

"Na gold for Port Harcourt e," he said.

"Hi be like say make I know go again."

"Haa! *My broder, I go happy."*

"Beautiful environment," I added.

Effects of crude exploitation

"Na so everybody dey tok when dey come here," Poweigha reflected thoughtfully. *"Na hin make government no leave us alone. We dey tell dem say even if dey wan take dem oil, make dem take am make dem leave us alone. If to say you come here when dey spoil dis place with oil, you go pity us my broder. All di place wey you dey see so, na so dey take oil cover everyting. Come see as fish dey die. No be Ukubie I run come?* (Turning to Eseimokumo and the principal for confirmation.) *And di oil, after dey take am away, we no dey see anyting, I know say God go answer our prayer one day,"* he concluded , stretching out his open palms symbolically, and laying them face-up in resignation over his knees.

I tactically withdrew from the subject. It was a good thing Kekemeke was not with us or within earshot; it would have been an occasion for him to resume his vituperations.

Funkeye and Fineface never relented; they stayed with us to the very end of our stay, prompting us at every turn to renew our pledge to come back for them. We handed them a few Naira notes. They thanked us profusely and told us they would be expecting us.

The trip home was as pleasant as our stay in Koloama. The tide was in our favour, hence the boat powered effortlessly back home. The ride was so smooth that Samuel and I even took turns behind the wheel. We stopped at e few fishing ports, including the one where we bought fish and *apopo gaari.* Kekemeke's wife had not returned, which was a great disappointment for him. He kept a sombre look throughout the return trip. At Lobia we stopped to buy a few items like meat, which were very rare to come by in Ukubie. We bought a live alligator and some snails.

It was an effort convincing the woman who sold us the alligator to take money. She wanted to batter it for palm-oil, but the good intervention of a man who promised to sell her palm oil saved the day for us. We finally got back to Ukubie around seven o' clock in the evening.

CHAPTER THIRTEEN

"Good afternoon gentlemen. Sorry to have taken you away from your regular schedule. The meeting is going to be very brief. I have called you to help me welcome an august visitor. As you can all observe there is a strange face among us. I guess he may not be totally strange to many of us as he is not new in the environment. This is Mr Pere Armstrong. He is also a teacher from a neighbouring school. Gentlemen, Mr Armstrong has been appointed the Supervisor for West African Council Examinations (more popularly known by its acronym, WASCE), for our school this year. (*General Applause*). I pray for your fullest cooperation for the period he will be here with us to carry out his duties."

These were my opening remarks at a staff meeting I summoned to welcome Mr Armstrong, the WAEC examiner posted to Government Secondary School Ukubie, to supervise the WASCE, after which I called on Mr Armstrong to address the meeting. In his address, which turned out to be a sermon, he dwelt extensively on the virtues of being honest and the long-term effect of cheating. After his speech, I allowed three speakers, Chief Abraham and two other teachers to respond. Even though they did not counter his admonitions directly, the trend was not an outright acceptance of his entreaty. Chief Abraham in particular made a distinction between internal and external examinations: for him, internal examinations call for strict control, while external examinations by their nature are removed from the control of school authority. His speech received an especially firm support from other teachers, for they egged him on with comments and cheers. I never read any ulterior meaning to the whole exercise. The meeting wound up on a cheery note.

The task of supervising the WASCE was foisted on me midway into the second term. The principal uncharacteristically had called at our regular draught session. Hitherto, he had never shown or demonstrated any interest in the draught affairs. The closest he had ever moved near it was that any time he was passing by he would stop just long enough to exchange greetings with us, and if he needed to see anybody in the group, he would stand at some distance and call the attention of the person. At times he could say something like: "if you are busy right now you can see me later." Naturally the person concerned would leave immediately. He had invited me in that fashion on one or two occasions. But one evening, he not only called at the session, but actually requested for a seat. We were all delighted to have him with us, and as usual, we resumed our regular jokes.

"Sir, can you see the *yeye* man you employed?"

"I have no idea he is like this," the principal said, his joke attracting a wide applause.

"Play! *iti,* your job is on the line," I hollered, after making what I thought was a winning move.

"I got you! *Oga, if I lose dis game no pay me dis mont salary,*" Teneni my opponent said, turning to the principal.

"*Egberi fa e*! There goes your May salary," I said as I closed the game with a winning move.

"Salary! He lost his your job already," the principal said as he bounced off his seat to add a punch to the joke, and the whole group went wild in a fit of hilarity.

"*Amoo! Amoo!*" Teneni quivered.

At some point the principal ordered drinks, and as if planned, the vice principal went home, and brought some snacks of *apopo gaari* and smoked fish.

Later in the evening, the principal came to our apartment to inform me that he would be travelling out to some far away school to serve as WASCE supervisor, and that he would be handing over the school administration to me. When I told him his vice principal was the proper person to hand over to, he went on to inform me that the vice principal would also be going out for the same exercise. He laid an especial emphasis on the need for vigilance and close monitoring, which are regular demands in any test or examination situation, the meaning of which at that point I did not realise. I was to appreciate his anxiety in a very painful manner.

Under the system I was familiar with, when teachers go out for such an exercise, they do not generally leave their duty posts for the entire period; they come back to their school and still perform some of their regular duties as the exercise allows. But the geography of the area and its attendant transportation problems did not allow this here! Once a teacher went on such an assignment, he stayed over there for the entire period. And in this particular case, the principal only came home once or twice to attend to salary matters, while the vice-principal never came home at all throughout the entire period—a period of about one and a half months!

I assumed the responsibility without any formal proclamation. I crept into the leadership saddle by practice and assumption. The principal never informed the teachers—to the best of my knowledge. With the absence of the principal and his deputy, in order of qualification and probably seniority, Samuel and I were next in line, but for some unprofessed reason the principal in practice had projected me into some prominence that would make me more eligible. For instance, I was the assistant games master (a post for which I drew an additional allowance of N25.00); I was the examination coordinator, another position that had earned me a public commendation from the principal. Added to these, my role in the boycott had given me an undeclared leadership position among the staff, so with the principal and his deputy away, the teachers naturally gravitated towards me for advice and direction.

An event took place which finally put a seal, though informally, over my leadership position. A member of staff lost his son in some pitiable condition. As soon as I heard of it, I mobilised members of staff to donate money for him, and to pay him a condolence visit as a group, a practice they had never witnessed before. At the member's house, I led them in prayers, gave a speech on behalf of the group, and left before the entertainment. And that was it: I became the acting principal.

The Invigilator, Mr Armstrong, a teacher from a neighbouring school and a former Sergeant-Major in the Biafran army, took his job with utmost enthusiasm and seriousness. Ever since I first introduced him to the staff, he had taken an especial interest in me. Each time we met, he always had something to tell me either about his immediate assignment or about his personal social life or his army experience. He was never short of anecdotes and aphorisms to drive home his claims and arguments. His philosophy of life was "do what you think is right, and let people do the rest- condemn or approve." He would always end by saying you could not do both.

The examinations started with the Practicals, during which my role was minimal. I did not go beyond handing out materials, after which I withdrew and allowed subject teachers to stay with the supervisor. However, on the day of Practical Biology, the supervisor informed me very early that the students would be working with rats, so I instructed form one students to go into the bush to hunt for them, but Parabida, the Biology teacher, insisted that the candidates should do the hunting themselves. When I pointed out the irregularity in such an arrangement to him, he not only took offence, but was raving all over the place that I was out to destroy the future of the students. I put my foot down, and insisted that not only would the candidates have nothing to do with the collection, they must not know anything about the specimen.

The supervisor took up the rest of the fight, and gave Parabida the full length of his tongue. Earlier on, I had encountered some opposition from the same teacher when I drew out a timetable for members of staff assisting the invigilator. I had made sure in the schedule that individual teachers did not supervise the subjects they taught, but Parabida would have none of it. He would rather want individual subject teachers to go in only for their subjects. For him, there was even no need for any timetable. Only a few teachers supported me, but with Mr Armstrong on my side, I got my way.

Trouble started the first day of theory papers. It was Bible Knowledge, an afternoon paper. As usual, I handed over examination materials to the supervisor, and went home to have my lunch and observe the afternoon siesta. I was still in the middle of my meal when a student rushed in to announce my attention was urgently needed by the supervisor. The message was delivered in a very serious tone, so I pushed aside my food and rushed to the examination hall. Nobody needed to tell me that something serious had happened. The supervisor was on the corridor, his briefcase in his hand, and ready to leave.

"Hello sir! Anything the matter?"

"Your students are not ready for the exam."

The stern look on his face further increased my fears.

"Not ready? How? What do you mean?"

I went past him and entered the hall. There, the students sat peacefully in their individual desks. As I stepped into the hall, the assisting supervisor, a teacher who operated in the junior classes mostly, stood up from a desk he had occupied, and moved towards me. I could not see any sign of unpreparedness anywhere in the hall. Everything appeared normal. I looked vacuously up to the teacher and the supervisor in turn for a proper fill-in. The teacher would not talk, but simply shifted his eyes away from me.

"Look, I told your students to take away their books, but they refused. I am not here to give a lesson but to invigilate an examination," the supervisor, who had joined me in the hall, said.

With that the picture became clear. All the students, with the exception of a girl, Sister Catherine, as I used to call her, had their lesson notes and textbooks flagrantly displayed on their desks. Some even had the audacity to bring in dictionaries. Gradually the gravity of the situation began to dawn on me. The situation appeared very dicey. First, the examination must be conducted, and second, like the supervisor, I was not going to be a party to the cheating intended by the students.

"I told them this man will not cooperate, but they won't listen" the teacher whispered to my ears.

"Cooperate! or what did you say?" I looked at him with all the scorn I could muster.

"Good afternoon students, I hope we all know why we are here?" Not a single one of them responded, even after I repeated the question. I there and then decided that I would need more firepower to assert my authority. I gave more gravity to my voice, and went on full blast:

"I will like to remind you, in case you have forgotten, we are here to write West African School Certificate Examination, and it is a generally known and respected etiquette of examination that you do not bring in notes, textbooks or cribs of any type. I will appeal to the supervisor—here I turned to him bowing in respect to which he acknowledged by bowing in response—to give you ten minutes to take out all notes, textbooks and dictionaries out of this examination hall. However, if you refuse to do so, I will have no power to prevent the supervisor from leaving."

With that I moved out of the room to the corridor to let off steam. Midway into my speech a boy, the most brilliant in the class, had stood up and was about to move his books out of the hall, apparently in response to my instruction, but I stopped him with a loud shout. He dropped his books, and sat down as if he had come in contact with a hot object. I knew he had good intentions, but I needed to do so to assert my authority. Shortly, the supervisor joined me on the corridor. Samuel had arrived half way into my speech and he came in and perched over a desk. His arrival added a little bite to my voice. He joined us on the corridor as I started reviewing the situation with Mr Armstrong.

"What type of jungle is this?" Samuel remarked.

"Please, hang around for the next ten minutes, if they comply you can go on with the exam and if they do not I will gladly endorse your report."

The student who had earlier attempted to move out his books came out and dropped his books tamely on the corridor, moved towards me and said:

"Sorry sir."

"That's alright," I answered without looking in his direction.

In ones and twos, the students came out to the corridor to drop their notes and books. After the last of them had done so, we moved in and conducted a thorough search of the entire hall. After we were satisfied that the hall had been totally rid of notes and books, we turned to individual students to conduct a personal search, which yielded a few cribs. I then turned to the supervisor as if I was making a formal report:

"Thank you sir. I think the students are now prepared for the examination. Sorry for the inconvenience."

The examination went ahead, smoothly. Both Samuel and I stayed around to assist the supervisor. Even though we had succeeded in taking care of the immediate problem, I knew we had a battle on our hands, and that what we went through that afternoon was just the tip of an iceberg, the beginning of a long and protracted struggle. Mr Johnson, the assistant supervisor, seeing that we had our way, changed his earlier wait-and-see attitude, and warmed towards us. As we left the hall, he ran towards me, and congratulated me for a job well done.

"*Oga you try e.*"

"Not me alone. All of us did it."

"You no see as I dey look before you come. I don determine say if anyting happen, na window I go take comut"

"Nothing will happen. Even if I am the only person left, they can't remove a hair from my body."

"Dis boys! You try e. Penane no fit do wetin you do dis afternoon".

"The principal?"

"I teeell you."

"Even you, can do it if you are determined"

"For where? Na only me my mama born."

"There is nothing to fear."

"Dis oga go finish dis invigilation so?

"He has started, and he will finish it and nothing will happen to him."

"Make God help am e."

I knew he was not sincere in his remarks and comments, but I kept egging him on, knowing full well he would later report everything to some quarters—students and members of staff alike. I wanted him to go away with the impression that I was up to the task and battle-ready. I was indeed taking advantage of the erroneous impression common among the indigenes about Yoruba people—that is, that every Yoruba man and woman had powerful charms and supernatural powers.

After seeing the invigilator off, we settled down to review the situation. It was satisfying to know that Samuel did not show any sign of apprehension, which gave me all the courage I needed. We had planned earlier on to pay Benedict a visit that evening, but we had to shelve the plan for obvious reasons. Paying Benedict a visit meant walking the length of the village, and in the dark. We might be exposing ourselves to unnecessary reprisal attack from the students. The supervisor too said something along that line when he was leaving.

By 9:00 pm Benedict showed up at our house to inform us about the cataclysm going on in the village. My name was on every lip. I had connived with the supervisor to destroy the future of the students. He was very happy that we decided to call off our visit to his place. He was surprised to see that we were very calm, that even his report of the situation in the village did not in any way alarm us. He advised us to be careful the way we handled the rest of the examination, and the way we moved around in the community.

Consequent sessions went without any major incident. The students, at least to the best of our knowledge, no longer openly brought textbooks or written materials into the examination hall, even though we periodically had course to confiscate notes or cribs. No member of staff had the courage to confront me openly. It was however clear they were all disgruntled an unhappy with us. Occasionally, however, some teachers came in brazenly to assist the students. A very good case of such occurred during the Biology Objective session. The subject teacher, Mr Parabida, came in with a prepared answer sheet, which Samuel artfully seized from him. Going through the answers, I found out two or three wrong answers, and I decided to capitalize on the fortuitous discovery. At the end of the paper, I called the students' attention to the wrong answers by reading out the particular questions and asking them to give the correct answers. I later pointed out to them the wrong answers their teacher had intended passing on to them. Even though the students were not impressed—as I had hoped, judging from the ever present belligerent and hostile look they wore—I knew I had made my point.

The closest any member of staff came to discussing the issue with me was when Chief Abraham, in an offhand manner, remarked that one could prevent cheating in an internal examination, but students could be left alone or even given guidance in an external examination situation. When I asked him the wisdom behind the double standard, he cleverly eased himself out of the discussion, and never mentioned it thereafter.

Midway into the examination, on a Saturday morning, Ebitonye came with some fresh fish, ostensibly to ask if we would buy. She actually came to brief me about the developments about the examination imbroglio. According to her, the students had been having a series of meetings to deliberate on a possible line of action. While few of them were bent on taking drastic measures like manhandling us, a good number of them were against such actions. The general feeling was that they should resort to individual surreptitious actions like bringing in cribs, hiding notes on their persons and writing notes on palms and thighs. She left with a plea that I should ease up on our actions. What she did not tell me, but which I eventually got to know, was that she was actually approached by the students to appeal to me for leniency, as the informant described it. I also established lines of interaction with quite a good number of the students, which gave me valuable access to their thinking and whatever action they were planning to carry out.

The most intriguing drama happened on the day of Mathematics Paper II (Theory). Ever since I discovered the nefarious intention of the students, I had made it a point of duty to be present at the examination hall. If I was not there I ensured Samuel was in attendance. On this particular day, we were there together with another teacher. I personally distributed the question papers, which the invigilator counted before he handed them over to me. When it was time to ask the candidates to start, a student, who sat by the window raised up his hand to complain that he had not been given the question paper. I was sure and could swear I had given him one. I could remember even chatting with him after giving him the question paper. At first, we decided that we were not giving him another one, and asked him to retrieve the earlier one wherever he must have kept it. So far, the impression I had was that he simply wanted to have an extra question paper, but the motive later became clear. After much consideration, we gave him another one, and the examination started. About fifteen minutes into the paper, we started receiving missiles of rolled pieces of paper flying into the hall through the windows. The first one I picked was the worked answer to question number five. This was a new dimension and there was little we could do to stop the inflow, but we ensured none of the missiles got to their intended targets.

By the end of the examination, a paper of two and a half hours duration, we had collected a basketful of cribs. The picture then became clear: the boy who had claimed that he was not given the question paper had actually passed the first copy he was given through the window to some external agents, who were preparing answers to the questions, and sending them in bits to the examination hall through the windows.

A few minutes to the end of the paper, when the inflow of cribs had ceased,

I asked the invigilator to join me in a walk around the neighbouring classrooms. Our find was intriguing, and at the same time interesting. There, in one of the classrooms, was a middle-aged man surrounded by a group of boys, mostly form one and two students. The chalkboard was full of worked answers to the examination questions going on some classrooms away. On sighting us, and possibly knowing what our mission was, the man got up, and before we knew what was happening, he bolted out through one of the windows—but not with his threadbare portfolio and his bowler hat, which fell off his head as he scaled the window frame. The junior students too took off in different directions. We were too stupefied to even attempt to apprehend any of them. We confiscated his left-behind bag, which was a stockroom of questions: past, present, and future. As we later found out, he was not a new person in the area. He was a regular visitor to Ukubie during WASC examinations. He was so regular that some village folks even thought he was a regular WAEC official. Much later, when I reflected on the incident, I thought he did us a great favour and honour by running away, because, judging by his physique and bearing, he could have easily taken care of the supervisor and me if he had waited to confront us. And even then, if we had succeeded in apprehending him, I could not think of what we would have done with him, for the nearest law enforcement agent was several miles away in Yenagoa, a twelve-hour boat ride to Ukubie.

As the examination progressed, most of the students gradually dropped their combative posture and, accepting the reality of the situation, gave up on trying to cheat. Some of them even threw banters at us during and after examination sessions, and at every turn we kept on sermonising on the virtues of honesty and self-reliance. Most of the teachers trying to assist the students gave up when they found out we were unyielding in our resolve to prevent any cheating. One obvious conclusion that we arrived at after seeing the contents of the portfolio of the mercenary examiner was that most of the students, if not all, had foreknowledge of most of the papers. But there was nothing we could do about that. We limited ourselves to ensuring that nobody brought in any texts or prepared answers to the examination hall.

The penultimate Saturday to the end of the examination, the principal came home, and naturally, I gave him a report of what had happened since he left. I briefed him on our experience with the WASC examinations.

"I heard everything. The news came to me over there."

"You mean somebody left from here to inform you?"

"Both teachers and students reached me, I am happy that you were able to do what I have been preaching over the years.

"But you gave me no warning in any form."

"I didn't have to. I knew you were up to the task."

"You didn't even bother about our safety?"

"I knew you would handle the situation. Warning you in advance would have served a negative purpose. Congratulations and thank you." The principal said and extended his hand, which I quietly took.

A day or two earlier, the students had handed me an invitation card to a send-off ceremony organised by the out-going class five students, the same students we had engaged in a running battle for the previous one month. I dismissed the idea as a rude joke, and threw the handwritten invitation away somewhere in my bedroom as soon as I had derisively gone through it. I was not about to expose myself to any mockery or physical assault. When I told the principal about it, he reached for his own on his table, allayed all my misgivings about the invitation, and told me he too would be there. Even with his assurance, I still was not convinced I should be there.

The remaining examination sessions went without any incident. The day of the party came; we decided not to attend because the principal had not arrived, we thought it might be dangerous to venture into the venue without him around. I had even had assurances from members of the class who were close to me, but I still decided I should be on the safe side. The party was supposed to start at five o'clock in the evening. At six o'clock, the principal breezed in and sent for us immediately. Given the enthusiasm and gusto he exuded, we decided to accompany him. The levels of friendliness and warmth the student displayed was simply unbelievable.

We entered the hall in the middle of a dancing session, but as soon as the students spotted us, the whole hall erupted in wild jubilation. The whole hall stood up and started clapping as we made our way to the seats already prepared for us at the high table. After the ovation had subsided, the senior prefect got up to welcome us formally. I listened carefully, expecting to detect any sign of trouble, but there was nothing negative in his words and actions. He was full of praise for us, and expressed the class's gratitude and happiness for honouring their invitation. We were lavishly entertained. I did not for once lower my guards; I still expected that trouble was locking somewhere around the corner.

However, all my fears were totally allayed when it was time for drama presentation. The senior prefect, who was the MC, had announced that they had some drama sketches. A feeling of anxiety descended on me because, given my cat and mouse relationship with the students over the examination entanglement, it intuitively occurred to me that I was going to feature in the forthcoming burlesque. The first one was a parody of the Mathematics teacher. It started with the teacher solving an algebra equation on a chalkboard. It was obvious he was having problems solving the equation on the board. In the middle of this confusion, a boy asked what appeared to be an honest question. The teacher suddenly turned to the class, which was represented by the whole gathering, and started accusing his students of not paying enough attention, pouring abuses and invectives on the boy who asked the question and the whole class. The teacher suddenly collected his books and lesson notes from the table, and walked out on the class.

"If you are not grateful for the wonderful job I am doing for you, I don't see why I should continue with you," he said as he matched out of the classroom.

The class saw him out with boos and catcalls. Other sketches followed and soon, it was my turn. Most of the drama sketches were non-complimentary, to say the least. As the skit on me progressed, the principal, who sat by my side, was quietly running commentary for us on the high table, filling the gaps and supplying details about teacher characters involved, which he did with so much adroitness and handiness that one could almost conclude that he must have rehearsed with the students.

The boy who acted me did it so perfectly that you could not mistake the representation. The character representation was so noticeable that the whole gathering erupted in laughter instantly as he appeared on the stage. I could not help clapping too. He dressed exactly like me, with my popular T- shirt and a shoulder bag I always carried around. I could not help clapping when in the middle of the class he said: "No! No! No! Leave your dictionary alone. Let's see if we can find out the meaning of the word by looking closely at the context"- complete with the right tone and genuflection. There was no mistaking who the subject was; all attention was on me. Strangely, no reference was made to the examination, a display of maturity I never expected from the students

When it was time for speech making, I at first refused to say anything, but with the principal's prompting, I got up to give a very short one. I thanked the class for providing such an avenue for us to interact after the strained relationship of the previous weeks, and then went into what turned out to be a rehash of the admonition talk I gave the class when the problem of cheating was brought to my attention for the first time. It was well taken, but I could still hear some background murmur and some faint catcalls from outside. I rounded off my speech by wishing them good luck as they stepped into the world. We left the gathering after the principal's speech, which in effect was commendation for me.

If we went scot free from the examination imbroglio, Mr Armstrong, the supervisor was not so lucky. The morning after the party, news came to us that while we were at the party, some unknown persons had gone into his room and made away with all the valuables. What they didn't take away they vandalised. When we got to the Chief's house where he had gone to lodge a complaint, we saw him, a pitiable sight. He raved and raged as the Chief assured him he would do everything within his powers to bring the culprits to book. We did all we could to console him. He would not accept clothes and other relief materials we put together for him. He left with the next available boat, swearing never to step on Ukubie soil again.

CHAPTER FOURTEEN

The month of July came, and it was time to bid Ukubie farewell and leave for the camp for the passing-out parade. Send-off parties were organised. As the day of departure drew near, I began to realise the depth of my attachment to the community I had loathed at first sight, and sworn never to have anything to do with. We had just returned from the party organised by the school, and I laid on my bed looking into space, while I took stock of my sojourn in Ukubie within the last eight months or so. My initial truancy and escape to Lagos, the Ebitonye phenomenon, my mercurial relationship with the principal, the boycott and a host of others laid before me like a canvas of mosaic oil painting. The characters, too, came before me in a strip of imagined apparition: Samuel; my Ukubie brother, for that was how everybody referred to him anytime we were not together and there was the need to refer to him; my estranged friend, Chief Benaebi; Ebitonye; Penane, the principal and his assistant, Mr Tamuno, and so many others. It suddenly occurred to me I was going to leave all of them for good. A feeling of cold, numbing consciousness, akin to the kind I felt on the jetty the day we arrived Ukubie the first time, descended on me. I could not believe what was going on. It was as if there was a second me in the room, and I was merely empathising with him. A feeling of some unusual warmth around my eyes brought me back to my senses. Wells of tears had formed around my eyes. "*O ga o*", I said loudly as Samuel sauntered into my bedroom to inform me about our travelling arrangement.

The information Samuel came with was bad and at the same time good. We had been told earlier on that we would be travelling in the school boat, but the principal had just called him to say that the boat had broken down on a trip to Lobia market. The boat had taken his wives to Lobia to get some supplies, but developed engine trouble on its way back. It would take one or two days to fix it, which meant that our departure would be delayed for a day or two. In a way, it meant we would be arriving late to the camp, but on the other hand it translated to more days with our friends, which was good news. We relaxed and deferred all last-minute packing. As school was no longer in session, our draught sessions became more robust, and took the best of our time. It started as early as ten o'clock in the morning and at times went far into the night. On a particular night, the principal had to send us his gas lamp.

Ebitonye travelled out to visit her relations in Cameroun a day into the extra time. She was to leave a day after our departure, but since the earlier arrangement had changed, it meant she had to leave me behind in Ukubie. I missed her. On the third day, the principal came with another bad news: the mechanics repairing the boat were not making any headway; he therefore advised that we leave in a hired dinghy. We doubted his claim, but since we had no alternative, we acceded to his plans.

Ever since our encounter with Mr Addey, the official from the NYSC secretariat, we never bothered to give the experience a thought, but now that we would be reporting at the secretariat, we thought it proper to fashion out a defence strategy in case he had given a damaging report to the office. An indictment at the secretariat meant we would be coming back to Ukubie for extension. We ruled that out; it would never happen. If it came to that, we would just abandon the whole NYSC exercise and leave for our respective homes. Whatever the situation was, we vowed to mobilise all the resources at our disposal to give Addey a fight of his life.

Exactly ten o'clock in the morning, our boat operator, Luke, arrived to move our luggage to the jetty with the assistance of two hefty boys. Our house was like a bus terminal; everybody was there to see us off. Together we trekked the ridge path to the jetty. It was a sharp contrast to the one that took us to the school compound the day we arrived. There were too many people and too much to say.

"Make you no say as post office no dey here, you no go write e." It was Teneni my second in command in the draught group.

"Why now? I will write," I replied as I gave him a soft pat on the back. *"I don tell you any lie since I don dey beat you here?"*

As we moved on, others who came late joined us on the way. Soon it was time for final greetings and handshakes. The emotions, which grew stronger as we moved closer to the jetty, became too much for some. The vice-principal just turned all of a sudden, raised his hands in goodbye, and went off, and never looked back. By the time the boat took off, it was only the strong-hearted, like the principal, who remained. The boat idled along in what we thought was an honour lap across the length of Ukubie. A few people along the riverside, students and locals, who knew we were leaving, waved us goodbye.

About ten minutes after takeoff, Ukubie was behind us, and yet the boat was still crawling. The movement was so slow that you could jump into the river, take a swim, and get back on board without much ado. We thought the operator was extending the honour ride a bit too long, so we requested for more speed. To our consternation, the operator tamely informed us he was going at the maximum speed. After one year in Ukubie, we were sufficiently familiar with riverine life and transportation to know that something was wrong. Even canoes move faster. We ordered him to go back immediately if he was sure the boat could not go faster. He tried as much as he could to let us know we were not going to get anything faster in Ukubie, but we insisted he should go back. He eventually took heed of our plea and made a U turn, and went back to Ukubie.

As we approached the village, we asked him to stop at the end of the village, near the house of Mr Parabida, a member of staff. We disembarked, and asked the operator to proceed to inform the principal about our predicament. A couple of minutes later, the principal showed up. He confirmed the operator's claim, brought out some new spark plugs, which he handed over to the operator. Ordinarily, we should have insisted on a better boat, which would have meant staying a day or two more, but the situation was in all ramifications loaded against us. First, we were already late for orientation camp, and second, we thought it would be an anti-climax to appear again in the village after the earlier grand and glorious exit, which was the reason we stopped on the outskirt of the village. With the assurance from the principal, and the operator's encouragement, we set out the second time.

A change of spark plugs at first seemed to give the boat a new push and appeared to make a difference, but after some time, it became obvious that nothing had really changed. We accepted our fate, and decided to make the best out of it. Perhaps if the trip had been a down-stream one, i.e., towards the ocean, it would have been more pleasurable, because there the river was wider and open. But going upstream meant going through the darkest evergreen forest ever, and most of the time against the current.

However, the mere fact that we were home bound gave us the courage to continue. The operator too turned out to be a very lively individual, and he did his best to relieve the boredom and weariness by cracking some jokes. At first, we did not pay him much attention, but in spite of that he went on, and even related to us an incident that took place during the examination debacle. It was how a group of students had approached a medicine man to help handle the invigilator and one stubborn teacher. He apparently did not know it was one of us that was involved, or if he knew, he made a very good job of concealing the fact.

"*So after dey don tell am how di inspector and di teacher no dey allow dem look inside deir book, and how he wan spoil dem life, he come ask dem wetin dey want make he do to dem,*" Luke continued his narration.

"*Wetin you go do wit di medicine man,*" I asked.

"*Me! No be my chop- chop I dey find?*"

"So what happened?" Samuel asked.

"*One of dem come say make hi kill dem.*"

"Kill?"

"*Yes e, but di man come say hi no dey kill person unless di person don kill anoder person, but before he even finish talk, his friend come say no be kill dem want. Dey want make di inspector and di teacher sleep anytime dey enter di place wey dem dey do exam.*"

"Jesus!" Samuel exclaimed.

"*Wait now! You never hear anyting! Di man come tell dem say, hi fit make only one person sleep, but if na two person na all di people wey dey inside di room go sleep.*" We all burst into laughter.

"What followed?" I asked.

"*My broder! As we dey laugh now, na so I dey laugh e. Na him di man come say make I go tanda for outside. Anybody sleep inside exam room for school?*"

"Nobody slept. In fact, I am the teacher," I added.

"*Gooooduu! See me see trouble! Na you?*"

"*Na me, but I no sleep.*"

"*Tank God! I know say he no do am for dem. Tank God. Who know say I go come see you like dis. Di sleep one even beta. Na di kill one worse pass. But oga if you sleep you no go no e. Na different person fit know*".

"*Shut up! Nobody sleep!*" Samuel said dismissively.

This was one of Luke's jokes that helped to brighten the otherwise boring journey. No serious incident happened except when we came across a medium sized snake swimming across the creek. Luke steered the boat to avoid it, but it came directly towards the boat raising its head as if in readiness for a fight. I got hold of the paddle lying on the bottom of the boat in readiness to strike the daring monster. But Luke tactically got the paddle from me, assuring us that the snake meant no harm. The wayward beast went round the dinghy in a half circle before it finally disappeared under some overhanging foliage. I later on remembered that it was a taboo to kill snakes among the Ijaw. Expectedly, Luke had his ever-ready epitaph to cap the experience. Snakes symbolize motherhood and good fortune, and hence should be treated with respect and humility. Later on, when we saw a dead one floating on the surface, he reverently threw something at it saying, "*I take dis one bury you*".

As the boat inched along the creek, it was increasingly becoming clear to all of us that we were not going to make Yenagoa, not to talk of Port Harcourt that day. It was a fact we all shied away from. When I summed up courage to ask Luke when he thought we would arrive at Yenagoa, he simply mused and shook his head.

"*We never reash Amasoma,*" he said after a long silence.

Whatever anger or frustration Samuel and I had remained bottled within us. Luke had done much to ward off any reprimand from us. Fact is, we considered him as a partner in distress rather than being responsible for our misery.

"Where do we pass the night," Samuel asked "I mean sleep?" He added when he read the empty look on Luke's face.

"*Small time we go reash Ogbembiri*".

"You know anybody there?"

"*Me,I no sabi anybody dere e, but if di Chief see your uniform, he fit allow us stay wit am for di night.*"

The Chief of Ogbembiri turned out to be a very fine and outgoing gentleman. If we had informed him of our coming weeks before, I do not know what else he could have done to ensure our comfort. He turned all the facilities and human resources at his disposal in full gear to ensure our comfort. A generator he had recently acquired was put on. The sight of his lit compound naturally invited some of his neighbours. Children too, came in their numbers. In next to no time, the Chief's compound was in a festive mood. Words had gone round that the chief was entertaining some important visitors. Men and women came in turn to greet us. Our NYSC uniform did the introduction. When I informed Luke that I wanted to change to something lighter, he advised against it. According to him, our uniform was the passport to all the hospitality we were getting.

As we later learnt, the Chief had just been picked among ten contenders for the throne, and the winning card for him was that he was well travelled, and so had connections in high places, a quality that would bring many good things to Ogbembiri. Our showing up, though fortuitous, was the beginning of better things to come, and the Chief was not going to allow the opportunity to impress upon the community the wisdom of their choice to slip. He spoke to us in relatively good English, and at times took the trouble to translate Pidgin English spoken to us by many of his visitors for effect. We took a cue from that, and never for once spoke Pidgin English, which we understood and spoke very well. Even Luke understood what was going on, and not only spoke to us in whispers to hide his Pidgin English, but also smartly transformed himself to some orderly or assistant, even complimenting us with some outlandish military salute.

Food and drinks were in abundance. Each time we had the chance to talk, we were careful to link almost everything with the Chief and the wisdom of Ogbembiri people for having the foresight of selecting an enlightened person like the Chief as their leader. The people were the more impressed when they were informed that I was from the West and Samuel was from the North. I never ran short of examples from Lagos, while Samuel too overawed us with wonder tales from Kano and Kaduna.

What otherwise would have turned out to be a good day ended on a sad note, when I discovered that I had left my shoulder bag containing a return flight ticket to Lagos, my purse containing a sum of eighty Naira and other vital items in Parabida's house where we took off the second time. I could hardly sleep during the night. Fortunately, when we were about to leave the following morning, we came across a chartered dinghy going to Ukubie. We sent a note through one of the passengers to Mr Parabida to send the bag through the operator on his return journey, which meant we would have to wait for the boat in Yenagoa. Late in the evening the operator came back with all the contents of the bag, except the purse and the cash. According to the operator, Parabida claimed some children found the bag and the contents floating on the river some distance from his house. Ironically, one of the items was a picture of Parabida in which he hid one hand inside the breast of his coat. He had given me the picture while we were waiting for the principal in his house. We thanked the operator, and boarded the last taxi cab to Port Harcourt.

Adjusting to city life did not come naturally. Boarding a bus at Diobu market was a Herculaneum task. We had problem keeping up with the fast tempo of commuters and cheeky bus conductors. The noise of traffic and the hustle and bustle of bus stops were too much for us. We wondered too if we didn't look weird. For the past eight months or so we had been each other's barber. Most of our dresses too have either gone undersized or faded.

We got to Diobu market around eleven o'clock by which time it was too late to start looking for any friend's house. We headed straight to NYSC secretariat, where we got the first shock of our life. It was a beehive of activities. It was bustling with life. The secretariat had been transformed into a transit camp, a place of reunion for corps members, who had been flung all over the Niger delta for the past one year. We alighted from the bus to the waiting hands of old friends. There had been much fretting and anxiety among our friends about our whereabouts. The general comment of friends was about how robust and well fed I looked. I got the confirmation when I stood in front of a full sized mirror in the lounge. I looked rotund and sturdy. Any subsequent stories about hardship and suffering in Ukubie never convinced anybody. The remaining part of the evening was spent telling and listening to stories of our experiences in our different areas of primary assignment.

As I laid down that night, I took stock of my Ukubie experience, and concluded I had not done badly after all, at least, compared to some of the stories I had heard. One particular colleague told the story of how he had been moved around the Oloibiri area three times, each move ending in one form of disaster or the other. At the end, he did not arrive at Port Harcourt with a pin of his belongings. He lost everything when a boat in which he was travelling capsized. He was lucky to have survived the accident. A fellow traveller with whom he had established some rapport during the journey pulled him along as he swam to safety.

In the hustle and bustle of the reunion, I took a special note of a remark by somebody that Mr Addey had asked about us. According to the boy, Addey had referred to us as 'Ukubie warriors'. Even though everybody had laughed over the odd label, the implication was not lost on us. We volunteered the story behind Addey's interest in us, and they were unanimous in their agreement with our action. As I laid down on a couch expecting Mother Nature to close my eyes for a deserved sleep, I rolled over the expression in my mind, juxtaposing all the possible interpretations, and marshalling all likely arsenals to confront each of the possibilities. Even though Samuel read the message as well as I did, he was as defiant as ever, and prepared for the worst as I was.

Unlike most colleagues, we had much to do at the secretariat the following day. We had not collected our allowances for the past six months. This was so because there was not much to spend money on in Ukubie anyway. We had subsisted on the foodstuff: rice, gaari, beans and palm oil, given to us by the school authority. In addition, when I was returning from my escape to Lagos, I came back with so large a supply of provisions that my estranged friend, Chief Benaebi, upon seeing the bulky luggage, asked if I was going into provision retailing business. I also had the twenty-five Naira monthly allowances I got from my assistant games-master position.

The following day, the first thing we did was to appear before the accountant to collect our outstanding allowance. When I mentioned the word Ukubie, the man looked at me as if it was a word forbidden to utter.

"Ukubie!

"Yes! Ukubie," I replied emphatically.

"You mean you have been in Ukubie without collecting your allowance?"

"Check your record," I retorted defiantly.

"Hey! My friends!" It was Addey from behind us.

"Yes we are. Or you don't want us to collect our allowance?" Samuel said before I could think of anything to say.

"OC!" I said derisively.

"You are welcome. Please follow me," Addey said in an uncharacteristic jaunty manner as he beckoned, and led us to an inner office.

"Let's collect our money first. You can do anything you want to do later!" Samuel protested.

"Please don't worry. Just follow me," Addey said pleadingly

The impression I got was that he was leading us to the Director's office where we would be handed the punishment for our impudence. The feeling was reinforced by the mournful look on the face of our friends, who knew about our encounter with him, and happened to be around at the time. We went past the Director's office, but he continued until he stopped before an office bearing a label carrying his name. When we entered the room, Addey sat us on the two guest chairs, and went on to bring his regular chair behind the table to join us.

On our way to his office, I had noticed some change in his carriage; he was not the pompous and scratchy Addey we encountered at Ukubie; he looked somehow tame and subdued, and this change of personality got me confused.

"Gentlemen, welcome to Port Harcourt. How was your trip from Ukubie?"

"Fine," I said. Samuel uttered some muffled sneer, but I quickly perched my palm on his thigh, gave him a mild pinch, and kept the hand there as a reminder for patience.

"Gentlemen I am sorry for what happened. I have been looking for you for the past one week. Everybody I spoke to told me they had not seen you," he said and went on appealing and trying to pacify us. "Ve... Ve Very sorry indeed," he rambled to an abrupt end.

"Addey you are one kind guy," Samuel managed to say.

"I ... sorry my brother," Addey said, giving Samuel a friendly pat on the back.

"I am happy at last that you recognize that we are human beings like you," I said as we got up to leave the room.

"Sorry! Eh….Please, meet the accountant for your allowance. If there is any problem let me know. Please...," Addey said apologetically, herding us benignly towards the door.

At the bursary, we felt the full weight of Addey's repentance and good will. The accountant abandoned everything else to attend to us. We completed the forms he gave us for six months salary arrears and withdrew to the lobby to chat with friends, who were also at the secretariat for one thing or the other. A few minutes later when we went back to collect our money, we were surprised when the accountant told us that we omitted the transport allowance. For each month, we were to claim transport allowance from Ukubie to Port Harcourt at the rate of N60.00 per month per person. On top of this was N25.00 for each month, which he branded inconvenience allowance. In the end, we collected almost double the regular amount. It was when we discussed the windfall with friends that we discovered that it was a special dispensation for the two us. We never had any qualms in taking this handout. Instead, we saw it as well deserved reparation for what Addey did to us and what we went through during the service year.

The passing out parade, as the last ceremony was called, turned out to be a non-event. Apart from the fact that corps members were so anxious to leave for their respective homes that they gave the ceremony no serious attention, a list of national honours awardees brought out the previous day infuriated everybody, for it was a directory of girlfriends and cronies of the NYSC officials under a stage name. A ceremony intended as a glorious end to a year of dedicated service to the nation turned out to be one of mild protest and demonstration. Corps members would not listen to the speech of the Director, which he was forced to abandon halfway amidst catcalls and boos. The State Governor, taking a cue from the director's experience, abandoned his prepared speech, and addressed corps members extempore, his half admonition and half exultation being practically drowned in shouts of *hi doo! hi dooo!! hi don doooo!!!*

EPILOGUE

Marooned in the Creeks: The Niger delta Memoirs is an account of a real life experience rendered in a fictionalized form. It is the diary of a young man on a national assignment under the National Youth Service Corp scheme. The narrative took place a few decades ago (1979) in the Niger delta area of Nigeria, specifically in the present day Bayelsa State of Nigeria. The one year service took place in the riverine community of Ukubie or Okobie, a short distance from the Alantic Ocean. As is obvious from the story, I never liked the idea the first time I discovered I was posted to the area and for this reason, I struggled unsuccessfully to effect a change of posting. Left with no alternative, I decided to make the best out of the situation. *Marooned in the Creeks: The Niger delta Memoirs* is the story of my struggle to make the best out of a bad situation.

In rendering this account of my experience, I necessarily have to account for how others related to me which may not necessarily tie with how the individuals perceived the interaction. To remove such rough edges of likely discomfiture, I have changed the names of major characters including mine. However, this disguise can only screen off readers who were not privy to the incidents and events of the story. For readers who were part of the story, no amount of masking can hide the identity of individual characters.

Where my point of view provokes any negative reaction, I crave the indulgence of such persons and beg for your pardon. I have told the story the way events and incidents as they occurred to me.

As much as I would have loved to, it has not been possible to maintain any relationship with Ukubie and many of the characters that feature prominently in this story. On getting back home I sent an avalanche of letters to Ukubie. I waited six months before a single reply came. It was from the vice-principal. We maintained contact for about two years. Ebitonye never got my letter until after a year judging from the tone of her reply which I got almost a year and a half after. I was to see her twenty years after under an excitingly fortuitous circumstance. She had not changed much, but she had married and developed into a cool graceful lady. Sadly too, I have not heard from my partner, Samuel. I misplaced his address, which I got from him when we parted. I sent a letter to the NYSC secretariat of his state of origin, but no reply came. I hope he is alive and doing well.

The National Youth Corp Service scheme is no doubt a noble and worthwhile scheme. It's relevance to national development and integration cannot be overemphasized particularly in a multi-racial nation like Nigeria. For instance, I do not know of anything that could have taken me to Ukubie or any part of the creeks where I spent the service year on a short visit not to talk of a one-year sojourn. As is obvious from my account, even though the idea of spending my service year there sounded most repulsive to me in the first instance, I got so used to the place and the people to the extent that I felt a strong sense of nostalgia when it was time to leave. Judging from my experience, I should say that the scheme needs some serious make-over in the area of welfare of corps members. A case in point is the fact that even though we were not taking our monthly allowances for almost eight months, it never occurred to anybody in the secretariat to find out why. The only contact we had with any NYSC official was more of a combative penitentiary visitation than a supervisory call.

Perhaps I should also seize this opportunity to appeal to the authorities to give special priority to the development of the riverine communities to foster a sense of belonging. So strong was the sense of ostracism that we used to say we were going to Nigeria each time we were travelling out of the area. The fact that barter economy was alive and thriving in that part of the country in the last quarter of the twentieth century is an index of the neglect and remoteness of the area. I don't know what must have happened between then and now, but there was a strong and pervasive sense of abandonment among the people. For example, the younger folks, mostly students, looked more to Cameron than to Nigeria, at least, judging from where they preferred to spend their holidays. Extending common infrastructural amenities like roads, electricity, and communication facilities to the area will go a long way in generating a sense of belonging and improving the lots of the people.